As Rube steered his pirogue north and started back for Point Bleau, he felt the boat rise below him. It lurched a good two feet into the humid Louisiana air, then hit the water's surface with a resound splash. Rube forgot the oars and grabbed for his shotgun. He was in the act of jacking a shell into the breech when a great, leathery tail, as thick as a tree trunk and covered with algae and barnacles, rose from the swamp and lashed out. It hit the barrel of the Mossberg, sending the twelve-gauge spinning from his hands and into a dense clump of cattails. Then the tail continued to fall. Like an unyielding pillar of stone, it struck the pirogue squarely in its center, parting the sturdy dugout as if it was made of flimsy papier mache.

Abruptly, Rube found himself in the water. He kicked off his knee-high boots and began to swim for the sandbar he had just left. He was halfway there when he felt a heavy tug at his right leg. His heart played a symphony of dread as he felt himself sinking. A crushing pain gripped his lower body as an eighteen-foot demon began to haul him to the very depths of hell.

But, unlike the hell of his upbringing, it was not one of fire and brimstone. This hell was a decidedly liquid one, as cold and black as the womb of a dead woman.

TALES
FROM THE
SOUTHERN-FRIED
CRYPT!

RONALD KELLY

STORIES AND INTERIOR ARTWORK BY RONALD KELLY / COVER BY ALEX MCVEY

CONTENTS

BENEATH BLACK BAYOU

Reuben Traugott set off into the swamp in search of his brother, Lemuel. He took his most water-tight pirogue, a canteen of fresh water, a quarter pound of possum jerky, and a twelve-gauge Mossberg pump. But even as he headed across the dark waters, Rube knew deep down in his soul that he would never find his troublesome sibling alive.

Most who ventured into Black Bayou after nightfall never were.

The bayou held a dozen different dangers, perils that shunned the light of day yet emerged at twilight to swallow its careless victims whole. There were quicksand pools, poisonous snakes, and wild animals weary of rabbits and weasels, eager for a change of menu. The Cajuns even whispered of the evil La Sanguinaire, a species of demonic spider that trapped wayward swampers in its misty web and fed upon their life's blood.

And then there was Ma Gator. Old Ma was Black Bayou's resident man-eater. It wasn't known if the alligator was indeed a female or not, but the sheer fury of her constant attacks reminded the men in the area of a wrathful woman with an axe to grind. Ma was said to be well over eighteen feet long from toothy snout to scaly tail and close to a thousand pounds in weight. There was no record of precisely how many men had been killed by the gator, but there was speculation that the number had grown to nearly thirty-five since the mid-1950s. Usually the only thing found to mark a Ma Gator attack was the ruin of a canoe or pirogue floating upon the still waters and, occasionally, an arm or leg that had been severed by Ma's massive jaws and forgotten as she dragged the remainder of her catch to the muddy bottom of Black Bayou.

Rube headed out at daybreak, hoping to find some sign of Lem's whereabouts by afternoon, which would allow him enough time to make it back to Point Bleau before darkness fell. His brother had been a damned fool for taking his canoe across the bayou the night before, but then such behavior was to be expected of a man like Lem Traugott. The trapper was a notorious drunkard and wife-beater, and his indiscretions were what drove him from his home twelve hours before.

Lem had come in all liquored up and angry over having lost at poker. He had decided to take out some of the misery of his misfortune on his children rather than his long-suffering spouse. But Harriet Traugott had not taken kindly to that. She had grabbed an old scattergun from the corner and peppered Lem's britches with rock salt. Lem had lit out of there like a scalded hog. Cursing to the high heavens, he had untied his canoe and set off across the bayou. Harriet had expected him to show up in time for breakfast the next morning, shame-faced and sore-tailed, but he had not.

So, Rube was on the bayou looking for him. The swamper rowed his low, wooden boat slowly through gnarled columns of water-logged cypress. Sunlight was sparse, scarcely able to penetrate the upper layer of dense foliage and stringy Spanish moss that hung from the limbs overhead. By noon, Rube had drunk half his canteen and nibbled away most of the possum jerky, and still he hadn't discovered hide nor hair of old Lem.

It was nearing three in the afternoon and Rube was seriously considering turning back, when he spotted a gleam of sunlight on bare metal a hundred yards ahead. He rowed up next to a sandbar and found the rear half of Lem's canoe beached there. It looked as if it had been cut in half with a chainsaw. But Rube knew exactly what had done it. Only the snaggle-toothed jaws of Ma Gator could have torn the narrow boat so violently asunder.

He made a slow circle of the sandbar, looking for more evidence of poor Lem, but all he found was a splintered oar and his brother's soggy hat with a couple of crawdads walking around the brim. He yelled Lem's name several times, but to no avail. He found himself feeling a little foolish calling to a man who was probably in the process of being digested at that very moment.

"I am sorry, my brother," apologized the Cajun after uttering a silent prayer.

"But I must head on back without you. One Traugott for supper is quite enough for dat wicked bitch."

But Ma Gator wasn't so sure.

As Rube steered his pirogue north and started back for Point Bleau, he felt the boat rise below him. It lurched a good two feet into the humid Louisiana air, then hit the water's surface with a resounding splash. Rube forgot the oars and grabbed for his shotgun. He was in the act of jacking a shell into the breech when a great, leathery tail, as thick as a tree trunk and covered with algae and barnacles, rose from the swamp and lashed out. It hit the barrel of the Mossberg, sending the twelve-gauge spinning from his hands and into a dense clump of cattails. Then the tail continued to fall. Like an unyielding pillar of stone, it struck the pirogue squarely in its center, parting the sturdy dugout as if it was made of flimsy papier mâché.

Abruptly, Rube found himself in the water. He kicked off his knee-high boots and began to swim for the sandbar he had just left. He was halfway there when he felt a heavy tug at his right leg. His heart played a symphony of dread as he felt himself sinking. A crushing pain gripped his lower body as an eighteen-foot demon began to haul him to the very depths of hell.

But, unlike the hell of his upbringing, it was not one of fire and brimstone. This hell was a decidedly liquid one, as cold and black as the womb of a dead woman.

Rube Traugott awoke... but not in the belly of Ma Gator.

He found himself lying in two inches of rank swamp mud, surrounded by total darkness. He reached up and his hand touched the slimy stone three feet overhead. He was in some sort of cave... an underwater cave from the sound and motion of water lapping at the narrow opening to his left.

Trembling, he ran his hand down his belly toward his lower body and the sharp pulse of agony that had brought him back to consciousness. Relief flooded him as he discovered his right leg intact. It was cocked at a strange angle and broken in a place or two but was still attached to his hip. But what was he doing here? And why hadn't Ma Gator gorged herself on him during their frantic struggle near the sandbar?

Slowly, Rube's mind cleared, and he found that he had a pretty good idea. Gators rarely ate large game at a single meal. While the reptiles gulped down bullfrogs and swamp coons like popcorn, they preferred to take their time with larger critters. It was well known to the Cajun that a gator would sometimes drag a wild boar or small deer down into the depths of the bayou and stash it away in its underwater lair. There it would remain in storage, safe from rival predators, until the gator returned to consume it at leisure.

But there was something particularly odd about Ma Gator's latest catch. It was still very much alive.

Rube sat up and bumped his head on the cave's low ceiling. The man cussed and lay back down, propping himself up by an elbow. He breathed raggedly in the darkness and gagged on the cloying smell of stagnant mud and something else. He had to concentrate for a moment before he realized that the offending odor was that of decay. The creeping decay of something that had not been dead for very long but was turning sour mighty fast.

The swamper rummaged through his trouser pockets. All he had with him was his lucky buckeye, a black plastic Ace comb, a three-bladed Case pocketknife, and the old Zippo lighter he had carried around with him since the Army. He sat there for a moment, as if waiting for his eyes to adjust to the darkness, but no dice. There was no light to separate shadow from contrast, not even from the narrow mouth of the cave.

Almost reluctantly, he opened the lid of the lighter. He didn't really want to see the cramped conditions of his predicament or the putrid thing that shared it with him. But Rube Traugott was not a man to pussyfoot around when things looked bleak. He placed his thumb on the roller and struck the flint.

The flame licked up, casting a pale glow on the surroundings. The depth of the cave, from mouth to back wall, was about thirty feet. Gator dung and old bones lay scattered across the muddy floor. In the corner there was a broad nest constructed of wilted ferns and thick moss. Amid the hollow of the next were six leathery eggs. The unhatched young'uns of Ma Gator.

Then Rube turned around and the flickering light of the Zippo revealed the source of that godawful stench.

It was the body of his lost brother. Lem lay on his side, arms gnarled into fighting claws of fruitless rebellion, his pale face stretched taut into a rictus of horrible fear. Rube directed his light downward and found that his brother's body ended just below the ribcage. Ma Gator had bitten the poor bastard clean in half.

Rube was overcome with shock and nausea. He doubled over and vomited up that afternoon's jerky, as well as the sorghum molasses and biscuits he had eaten for breakfast. He tossed the Zippo aside and the blue-yellow flame winked out as the lid snapped shut on impact. Merciful darkness embraced him once again. But the smell—oh dear Lord, that confounded smell was still there, stronger than ever.

His brain boiling hot with panic, Rube scrambled for the narrow opening of the cave and squeezed through. Abruptly, he was surrounded by cold, black water. He struggled against the chill blanket of liquid limbo, bubbles of oxygen flooding from his mouth and nostrils. His eyes caught a glimmer of soft light from above and he knew that he was looking at the surface of Black Bayou. He kicked against the muddy bottom, pushing himself upward. An explosion of white-hot agony shot through his shattered leg, sending a wave of sickening dizziness through him. It seemed as though he surged toward the growing light for an eternity. Then his head broke through the barrier and he was back into the world of the living, back into *his* world.

But not for very long.

The first thing he saw when he reached the surface was Ma Gator. She lay on the sandbar, sunning herself in the last crimson rays of the Louisiana sunset. The splash of his emergence drew the reptile's attention. With a snap of horrid beartrap jaws, Ma bellied toward the edge of the sandbar and slid smoothly into the water after him.

Rube had no choice but to return to the dungeon from which he had escaped. He kicked and flailed wildly, diving deeper, ever deeper into the pit of murky darkness. He could feel Ma Gator behind him, getting closer, her huge tail propelling her forward like a leathery torpedo. On his way down, Rube wondered if he would even be able to find the cave again. He struggled with the twisted roots of a sunken cypress for one maddening moment, escaping from its tangle only seconds before the gator's jaws could grab hold.

Then there it was—the narrow mouth of the underwater lair. He pulled himself through and skittered across the mud and excrement to the back wall. His hasty entrance was followed by that of Ma Gator. She poked her huge head through the slit of stone, snapping and bellowing like an angry bull. He could not see the monster coming for him; it was much too dark. For some reason that was much worse than experiencing the horror close up and personal, the thought of not knowing when violent death would come to claim him.

He cringed against the rear wall, squeezing into a thin crevice that ran from ceiling to floor. He held his breath. He could hear the wet sound of Ma Gator crawling through the muck toward him. Rube felt something blunt and alive press against the foot of his injured leg and he knew that it was the reptile's probing nose. He cried out in fear and pain and pressed himself further into the crevice. As he did so, his hand brushed a long, hard object lying near the nest of eggs. His fingers enclosed the bludgeon. With a snarl of desperation, Rube struck blindly at the stalking gator, catching it across the snout. Ma bellowed with surprise and began to back away. He struck out again and again, driving the gator toward the mouth of the cramped cave. His other hand came into play and grabbed hold. Swinging the object like a baseball bat, he laid a stunning blow between Ma's beady eyes, or the spot where he assumed they were.

It did the trick. The alligator had had enough for now. She slid back through the opening, into the freedom of the open bayou. "Git yourself on away from here, you ugly she-bitch!" sobbed Rube. He collapsed against the floor of the cave and listened to the fading sounds of Ma Gator's retreat.

After a while, he gathered the will to get up. He scrambled around the cave for a time, searching for his discarded lighter. He finally found it. Once again, he snapped it on. The fluid-fed wick revealed the true nature of the weapon in his hand. The thing he had chased Ma Gator away with was the denuded leg bone of a full-grown man.

Rube laughed until he cried. "Looky here, dear brother," he cackled, waving the femur above his head. "Now wasn't dat a good one pulled on de old gator, do you not think so?"

Lem Traugott gave no reply. He only laid there and grimaced grotesquely at his living brother. Death had done nothing to improve Lem's sense of humor, which hadn't been much to begin with.

Despite the stink of the decaying body, Rube tenderly propped Lem's upper torso against the back wall and secured the Zippo in the stiffened fingers of one of his hands. He frowned in disapproval at the state of his brother's appearance. He pulled a couple of bloated leeches from Lem's unshaven cheeks and combed the mud-plastered hair carefully into place with the Ace comb. It helped to promote the illusion of life, but not very much. There was still that frozen mask of unspeakable terror seizing his brother's lard-white face. A terror that would remain, transfixed, for as long as the flesh was intact.

Hours passed. Exhausted, Rube slept, dreaming of he and Lem as children, of the coon hunts they had taken through the marshland and the Huck Finn raft of cut saplings they had constructed and poled all the way down to Baton Rouge.

When he awoke, he was hungry. The stench of decay had intensified, but that didn't seem to ruin his appetite. He lit the Zippo again, aware that the flame was growing shorter and dimmer with each use. He had no earthly idea whether it was morning or evening, noonday or night. He had no timepiece to consult with. His father had passed his pocket watch down to the elder Lem upon his deathbed. Whole lot of good it had done his brother, though. The big railroad watch was probably ticking its way through the maze of Ma Gator's bowels by now.

His stomach grumbled, pleading for nourishment. Slyly, he turned his eyes toward the nest in the far corner.

Rube crawled over and took one of the leathery, gray eggs in his hand. His fingers dug into the soft shell and a slimy residue erupted through the punctures. He could feel the small, warm body of a gator embryo loll against his fingertips.

"Eat me, will you, Ma Gator?" grinned Rube. "Maybe so. But a condemned man, he must have his last meal. And while you have a taste for man-meat, I have my own… for gator."

And, with that, he split the shell in half and swallowed the fetus in a single, savory gulp.

Existence in the gator's lair drew on, changing the shape of Rube Traugott's life, twisting it into something less than that of a human being.

By his estimate—which was distorted and imprecise given the circumstances—he had been holed up there for nearly four days. He had set his broken leg the best he could, using the discarded bones of Ma Gator's victims as splints and strips of cloth from his shirt to bind them with. The limb was crooked and stiff, but the sickening pain had reduced considerably, leaving only dull throbbing.

He found himself sleeping often, like an animal burrowed into hibernation. He had plenty of water to sustain him and outside air filtered from the narrow crack at the rear of the cave. While awake, he kept a fire burning using the Zippo and dry tender from the nest. Sometimes he sang the old songs and told the corny jokes that he and Lem had traded around campfires during their youth. But his was the only voice that rang through the cramped cave. Lem simply sat there, silent in his slow but steady decomposition.

Sustenance was the biggest problem. He had finished off the last of the gator eggs, as well as any slugs, insects, or leeches he could find in the cave. Despite the severity of his broken leg, he had tried several times to reach freedom. Each attempt, however, had proven futile. Ma Gator was always somewhere around, either laying on the muddy bottom near the entrance or swimming along the bayou surface, always aware of what stirred above and below her. Each time he would regain the safety of the cave, he would find his brother sitting there waiting for his return. And, as his hunger grew from nagging urge to cramping pain, Rube began to regard Lem not as a silent cellmate, but more and more as a side of meat that was rotting needlessly before his feverish eyes.

Once, Ma Gator had come visiting, gathering the nerve to return to the lair after the sound beating she had received at the end of a leg bone. Rube had been napping, when a great splash and a hoarse bellow shocked him from his slumber. He awoke just as Ma's massive jaws shot forward and clamped down. But it wasn't he who suffered the gator's attack, but his brother. The reptile snagged Lem's left arm and began to drag the corpse toward the mouth of the cave. With a scream of angry defiance, Rube reached for his brother's half-body, grabbing it around the neck. Man and gator fought for a solid minute, subjecting the carcass to grisly tug-o-war. Finally, the rope gave out. Lem's arm tore away at the shoulder with a moist rip. Satisfied for the time being, Ma Gator slipped back into the watery darkness, taking the limb with her.

Rube sat there, cradling his rescued brother before the smoldering fire. He held him close and sobbed with the abandon of a frightened youngster. Rube tried desperately to recall memories of he and Lem in the years past, the happy times they had shared along the mossy banks of Black Bayou. But no such recollections surfaced. There was nothing but the encroaching of primitive emotion, eroding away the remaining layers of civilized behavior from his weary mind. Soon, he feared, those dark emotions would grow so powerful that they would drive him toward total madness.

He hugged his brother's body closer, snuggling against it like a child to a battered teddy bear. As his tears began to play out and he drifted to sleep, Rube noticed that the awful stench didn't bother him nearly as much as it had before.

Rube knew that he must try for freedom once more—before the fine black worms of insanity burrowed too deeply into the tender meat of his brain and gained complete control.

"Farewell, my brother," he said, eyeing the pale form at the rear of the cave with genuine affection. Then he took the folding knife from his pocket and extended the longest and sharpest of the bunch. He would have much rather had a harpoon to defend himself with, but the lock blade would have to do. Taking a deep breath of stagnant air, Rube plunged into the dark waters and began his slow journey to the surface.

Halfway there, he met up with his nemesis. Ma Gator emerged from out of the murky darkness. She swept past and struck him a powerful wallop with a swipe of her tail. He felt ribs crack beneath the force of the blow. The impact and pain drove the reserve of air from his tortured lungs and he felt nasty water begin to snake its way into his nostrils and down his throat.

The gator made a sluggish U-turn and, again, came for him. He knew that there was nothing to do now but kill the monster or die trying. Motionlessly, he floated there, playing possum, lulling Ma Gator into a false sense of triumph. Then, as the gator's mouth opened to receive its prize, Rube surged up and over the lengthy snout. He found his intended target—the creature's left eye—and, with both hands, drove the blade of the pocketknife downward. The honed blade slid smoothly and without error into the gator's orb. Ma thrashed and snapped, but to no avail. Rube wasn't about to withdraw the knife from the fatal wound. Instead, he pushed harder, bearing down with all his strength, sending the blade past the occipital bone and into the brain.

Ma Gator jerked in a final, rolling spasm, then grew limp and still. Slowly, she began to sink downward toward the murky depths of Black Bayou.

Free! thought Rube Traugott. *Free from the fiend who imprisoned me!*

He began to work his way upward, toward the surface of the bayou and the bright warmth of daylight beyond. There life reigned eternal, full of love, hope, and laughter. Birds sang from leafy branches, hounds bayed and barked joyfully as they chased fox and coon, old men joked and gossiped on the porch of the general store, and young men asked demure ladies to share a dance at the tune of a Cajun fiddle and squeezebox accordion. Reuben Traugott would go back to his family and fish and trap and live the remainder of his years as a happy and contented man.

But the closer he grew to the shimmering surface, the more that idyllic life seemed impossible, even perversely absurd, in nature. His life beyond Black Bayou had ended in the depths of the gator's lair. It had come to a close with insanity's dark victory and the hideous acts he had performed by the light of a tiny fire.

Rube's heart pounded with panic, his brain swelling with horror as he came within a foot of bursting through. He swam there for a long moment, then began to ease back down into the comforting black depths. As the light of day faded into memory, he drifted to the soft mud bottom, letting the cold currents engulf him, letting the blind catfish and slithering swamp snakes caress his doubts and fears away.

Letting the loving embrace of Black Bayou welcome him home once again.

Emery DeBossier set off into the swamp in search of the Traugott brothers. He took his johnboat with the big 75-horsepower outboard, his
Winchester .30-30, and a Coleman lantern. He had no great expectations of finding Reuben or Lemuel, however. He knew Black Bayou and
its reputation well enough to have his doubts.

Unlike most men in Point Bleau, though, Emery was not one who
feared the twilight hours. He searched throughout the day and, when
dusk passed into night, he didn't seek the safety of the locked door or
the comfort of the woodstove. Rather, he ventured further into the far
reaches of the dreaded backwater bayou.

It was well after midnight when he made his discovery. Fragments
of both brothers' boats laid scattered upon a sandbar, like a graveyard
of ships that had chanced a perilous reef and fallen victim to its hidden
dangers.

He lit the lantern and steered his johnboat closer to the wreckage.

Suddenly, a gorge of water broke to his right and a long, leathery
tail arched through the night air. It hit the glass chimney of the lantern,
shattering it. Flaming kerosene splashed across Emery's face and hands.
Quickly and without a second thought, he plunged into the cold waters
of the bayou, dousing the burning flames before they could do much
damage.

The shock of the sudden dive cleared his head, bringing him to the
realization that he was in a very dangerous situation. He was about to
climb back into the boat when something grabbed his right foot. He
fought the best he could, but he was an old man and not as strong as he
had once been. He felt his fingers slipping from the smooth fiberglass
hull, betraying him, surrendering him to the thing that grappled with
him from below.

The cold black water rushed up to swallow him. He kicked and
flailed as the creature pulled him under. His knife! He had nearly
forgotten about it! Emery reached for the eight-inch skinner he carried
on his right hip. But it wasn't there. It had been—only moments ago. It
was as if someone had grasped the staghorn handle and pulled it from
the sheath mere seconds before he could get to it.

Deeper into the depths of Black Bayou he sank, the smothering
cloud of watery darkness engulfing him. Soon, he could fight it no
longer and found himself blacking out.

Emery DeBossier didn't expect to awaken, but he did. He laid there for a while, disoriented and confused. He seemed to be in some sort of cave—a cramped and dank cave underwater. But, strangely enough, it didn't seem like the lair of some marauding reptile. A small fire burned in the corner, casting an eerie glow upon the slimy walls of the cave, upon his shuddering and soaked form, and on the thing that sat nearby.

It was a skeleton. Or, rather, half a skeleton. Its bones were stark white and clean, as if it had hung in some college biology lab instead of moldering in the depths of a dark and muddy cave. Something about it disturbed Emery to no end. It was *too* clean. No animal could have done that. No animal could have picked the bones of flesh so meticulously and with such cunning precision.

Then, abruptly, the emphasis of Emery's terror shifted. The water at the mouth of the cave began to ripple and churn as his captor arrived. He cringed against the far wall as the great, toothy head poked its way into the cave. Emery could only watch, mortified, as the alligator crammed itself into the limited space. There was something vaguely strange about the way the gator moved, about the way its pebbled skin hung loosely on its body. But the Cajun did not give much thought to such things. All that concerned him at that moment was the dead-meat stench of the creature's breath and the mixture of malice and hunger that gleamed in its single, reptilian eye.

"Ma Gator!" he gasped as the horrid thing shambled closer.

"No," a familiar voice rasped in reply. "But you may call me Pa."

A hand appeared from a slit in the reptile's belly, an undeniably *human* hand, and in its grasp was the old man's missing knife.

It was then that Emery DeBossier looked into the gator's open maw and, from the innermost darkness, saw a grin within a grin.

OH, SORDID SHAME!

By the very nature and eloquence of this writing, few would believe that I was once a man enslaved.

That fact alone may cause some men to dismiss the validity of my story entirely, their suspicion of the negro race conquering their potential for open-mindedness. But the tale that this testament holds is truth. I swear by God that it is. Surely it might have remained untold for all time—and perhaps best so. But a dying man must purge his troubled soul. Therefore, I take pen in hand and cleanse my own of the stain of that horrid incident some sixty years ago.

I first came to know the name of Fontenot in the mid-1800s. Since my birth, I had been bound body, mind, and soul to the possession of another man... in fact, several over a twenty-five year-period. When gold had once again exchanged hands and I was bought by the family of Fontenot, I was a husband and father. Fortunately, the elder Fontenot was a man of compassion and not one to dissolve the family unit, putting so much faith and stock in his own. So, without ceremony, the three of us—my wife Camilla, my son Jeremiah, and I—were delivered to the Fontenot estate in southern Louisiana, near Baton Rouge. We arrived with the obvious fears and expectations, figuring to be cast into yet another dismal world of cane fields, slave shacks, and cruel overseers.

However, much to our surprise, life with the Fontenot family was nearly idyllic. Unlike our more unfortunate counterparts of dark descent, our servitude was pleasant and without conflict. There were no chains, no bullwhips, and never once did we hear the word "nigger" cross our master's lips. Since the Fontenot wealth was one of inheritance rather than the livelihood produced by sugar cane, the extent of the plantation and its grounds were simply there for the family's comfort and leisure. I was dressed in the finest of garments, taught the most impeccable of manners, and transformed from an ignorant field hand into a poised and proper butler. Camilla attended to the cooking and housework, while Jeremiah, then a small boy, took care of the stables.

Another benefit of serving the Fontenots was their uncustomary interest in our education. Phillip Fontenot and his wife, Catherine, possessed an immense library of both ancient and current volumes. All manner of books and periodicals were made available to us. While my former masters had deliberately kept my family and me in intellectual darkness—a common practice in the South during that period, generated more out of fear than hatred—the Fontenot clan seemed to encourage our pursuit of knowledge. The Fontenots' only daughter, Natalie, had hopes of becoming a schoolteacher someday and we were her first pupils. We became well versed in the classics, reading Dickens, Shelly, and Keats, and studying the histories and philosophies of the world. I would not be penning this testament this very evening if Miss Natalie's tutorial guidance had not left such a lasting impression.

And we were offered companionship as well. Camilla shared activities with Lady Catherine and Miss Emily, while I often went quail hunting with Master Sebastian and his eldest son, Jerome. And the Fontenots' youngest child, Oliver, was my son's bosom buddy. He and Jeremiah made the whole of the estate their private playground—climbing trees, skinny-dipping in the fish pond, and playing their favorite game, marbles, in the earthen circle drawn for that purpose beneath one of the garden's great, spreading magnolia trees.

So what went wrong? Why were we not allowed to live out the remainder of our lives in such a paradise, void of prejudice and strife? I have asked myself that question often over the years. Perhaps if I had paid closer attention, I could have foreseen the catastrophe to come. If I had not been so blinded by my loyalty to the Fontenots, I might have been able to do something to alter the course of events that led to the downfall of that most inoffensive and genteel of Southern families.

The history of the Fontenots was very much a mystery to me, as it was to most everyone in that part of Louisiana. From their accent and customs, it was obvious that they were originally of foreign lineage, most likely French. It was also known that the family had left their native country under the shadow of some great scandal. Sometimes, when partaking of strong drink, Phillip would slip and mention "exile" and some terrible "shame" that had forever tarnished the family name. He never elaborated on precisely what that shame was, only that it had taken place during wartime. My suspicion was that cowardice was the black mark of which he spoke, since Phillip and his family were of an overly reclusive and gentle nature. They had very little to do with the neighboring planters and whatever business was done in Baton Rouge and New Orleans was performed by myself. Jerome and Natalie had no interest in people their own age and never attended any of the dances or social functions prevalent during those days of antebellum grace. And young Oliver shunned the neighboring children, finding companionship only in the company of my own son.

The only other clue I had to the family's mysterious background was something I discovered in the Fontenot library. It was a journal belonging to one Almund Fontenot, grandfather to my master Phillip. Almund had been a man of medicine, a scientist in the purist sense of the word. He had been most interested in the workings of the human mind and the chemical imbalances that caused negative behavior, such as paranoia, anxiety, and, as in the case of his own heritage, fear and timidity. It was known that the doctor had developed a serum to purge future generations of such weaknesses. A few of the passages even hinted that Almund may have tested the concoction on himself. But from what I had witnessed of the Fontenot legacy, Almund's pursuit for genetic strength and stability had proven a dismal failure.

However, I did not allow their eccentricities to affect me. I respected the privacy they demanded and attended to my appointed duties. Camilla and Jeremiah did the same. For a while, things went pleasantly. Then a couple of incidents took place that were both puzzling and frightening to someone familiar with the mild nature of such people.

The first concerned Phillip Fontenot himself. He and his wife rarely exchanged hostile words; rather, they seemed most loving and considerate of one another. Yet, one evening, their customary civility gave way to a heated argument. It concerned Catherine's desire to enroll Natalie in a finishing school in Lafayette and Phillip's absolute refusal to allow the girl to venture from the solitude of the Fontenot household. The more Catherine pressed the matter, the angrier her husband became. His agitation was disturbing, for it was an emotion I had never seen grip the man before. I watched from the open door of the parlor as Phillip's face grew deathly pale. And there was something else. His eyes—the whites of his eyes had grown blood red. Not bloodshot like those of a drunken man, but pure blood red, only the pupils showing in stark contrast to the surrounding crimson orbs.

Phillip took a trembling step toward the lady, his hand aloft and balled into a fist. I am certain he would have struck her if I had not stepped into the room and drawn his attention. The man turned and regarded me with a fury that could only be described as murderous. At first, I thought he might take his anger out on me, but instead he stormed past, heading downstairs to the wine cellar. I followed at his urgent request and, soon, he and I were alone in the basement. There was an empty storage room at the rear of the dusty bottle racks, one with a sturdy oaken door and iron lock. He instructed me to lock him within the windowless cell and not come to release him until early the next morning.

My protests only seemed to feed the fuel of his madness even more, so I complied and did as I was told. The following morning I returned to find him crouched in a corner, his clothes disheveled, but his mind having regained its normal state of serenity.

The second event of this nature had to do with young Oliver. He was only five years old at the time and, even then, small and frail for his age. While he and Jeremiah were out cavorting near a neighboring plantation one day, they strayed upon a broad cow pasture. Halfway across, a great black bull appeared from a wooded thicket and gave chase. Both children reached the safety of the bordering fence, but the frantic run had played havoc with poor Oliver's nerves. By the time they returned home, the boy was overcome with fear and trembling. He was put to bed immediately. He developed a high fever the following day, but it did not seem to be from any form of sickness. Rather, it appeared that Oliver was in the throes of some bizarre temper tantrum, as if his initial fear had bled away into a creeping rage.

Later that night, while the household slept, young Oliver left his bed. Lady Catherine discovered the absence and alerted her husband. On horseback, Phillip, Jerome, and I searched the expanse of the estate, but found nothing. Then instinct nagged at me and I suggested we ride to the pasture where the bull had chased the two boys. As the dawn came, we reached the field and found the child lying in the dewy clover, his nightshirt torn and stained with blood. As father and brother carried the sleeping boy home, I lingered, wondering what had become of the mean-spirited bull. A short time later, I found out. The bull was sprawled in the wooded hollow, cold and dead. Its belly had been torn open and its entrails scattered throughout the brambled thicket.

Nothing else of such a morbid and inexplicable nature happened again for a very long time. Life with the Fontenot family continued as smoothly as it had before, leaving only uneasy reflections of the strange incidents to linger in the dark corners of my mind.

Then came the conflict between abolitionists and slave owners. The Southern states seceded from the Union, the Confederacy was born, and the great Civil War tore the fabric of normal existence asunder.

Men of all ages and social distinction enlisted to fight the Northern hordes that were sure to march across the Mason-Dixon line and put a halt to the ways of the Old South. The Fontenot men, however, did not. They remained neutral and refrained from the wearing of the gray. They were content to make the estate their private haven from war, intending to spend their time as usual—reading their books, hunting quail and fox, and living quietly and inconspicuously far from the roar of the cannons and the death screams of gut-shot soldiers.

They were ridiculed for their decision at first. Men rode onto the plantation in the dead of night and goaded them with curses and stones, calling the Fontenots "yellow-bellied cowards" and "Yankee sympathizers". During each episode of violent taunting, Phillip and Jerome were locked in the wine cellar, their eyes flaring like red-hot coals with each chiding word.

Eventually, more and more marched off to fight the war in Virginia and Tennessee, and fewer and fewer found time to torment the family who wanted no part in the conflict. By the second year, the plantations and sugar mills around Baton Rouge had grown quiet and deserted from disuse, and the Fontenots found themselves left alone, just as they wished to be.

And that was the way it remained... until a fateful night in the summer of 1863.

There had been much activity that day; the sound of marching troops and wagons on every road around the city and the roar of cannon fire from the direction of the Mississippi River. By nightfall, a division of Union calvary was galloping up the road to lay waste to any plantation loyal to the Stars and Bars. When the procession of flaring torches could be seen from the windows of the main house, Sebastian gave precise instructions as to what would be done. Rather than fight for their home and honor, he and Collin would retire to the security of the cellar as usual. The rest of the Fontenots, along with my family and me would hide in the upstairs parlor with orders to stay put, no matter what transpired.

I did exactly as I was told. By the time the males had been locked in and the women and children were secure in the mansion's upper level, I watched from the upstairs window as a group of cavalrymen invaded the Fontenot property, leaving the rest of the division to conquer other pockets of resistance.

No one will resist you here, I thought as the soldiers dismounted and marched boldly to the mansion's front door. *There is no one here but a few frightened women and children... and a couple of craven cowards hiding in the cellar.*

But I was wrong about that. Very wrong.

A Union colonel kicked at the door with his dusty boot. "Open up this door, you traitorous rebels, or so help me I'll burn this house to the ground with you in it!"

There was the sound of breaking glass, the steely rasp of drawn sabers, and the sound of wild laughter as soldiers—some drunk on confiscated spirits—began to ready themselves for the destruction of the massive structure of whitewashed wood and alabaster stone.

I looked to Lady Catherine. She was clearly frightened, but strangely enough, not because of the gathering of military men below. She held Natalie and Oliver in her arms, but the gesture did not have the appearance of a mother's loving protection. Instead, she seemed to be holding them in *restraint*.

The crackle of splintering wood echoed from somewhere downstairs. I was sure that the soldiers had breached the security of the locked and bolted front door. But, upon listening further, I discovered that the noise was too muffled to be coming from the ground floor. No, it seemed to issue from some lower level. From the shadowy depths of the wine cellar.

Then came the most horrifying wail of pure rare that I had ever heard in my life. It was fury torn between the mortal soul of man and the raw bloodlust of the most primal of beasts. It barreled up out of the pit of the mansion's black bowels, demanding to be vented, filling all who heard it with a fear so strong that it was as paralyzing as the venom of some exotic and deadly snake.

I turned and saw Natalie and Oliver then. Their faces were as pale as lard, their expressions contorted into a rictus of intense mental anguish. And their eyes... their eyes were the same shade of brilliant crimson as that which their father had exhibited that night so many years ago.

"I can't hold them any longer!" gasped Catherine, her slender arms surrendering the two struggling children. Natalie and Oliver ran for the door, their faces like those of demons, their hands curled into pale, fleshen claws. I moved to stop them, but the woman's voice cried out, "Let them go! Let them go or they will tear you apart!"

I stepped aside and they hit the door with such force that the lock was torn loose from its moorings. With enraged wails that more resembled the fitful snarling of beasts than that of innocent children, they disappeared down the staircase to join in the conflict below.

And what a conflict it was. There came another crack and splinter of wood, again from the inside. There was the sound of the main door being torn from its hinges and tossed aside. And there were screams.

Lord in Heaven help me, I can still hear those awful screams of fear and torment shrilling through the night air, climbing higher and higher, pushing the limits of the human vocal cords, then faltering into choking silence. Only a few gunshots rang out and there was the clatter of hooves on the flagstones as a few the horses escaped into the summer darkness. After the screams of dying men faded, all that could be heard was the maddening sound of flesh being ripped apart. That and the wailing chorus of earthbound banshees performing atrocities in the outer courtyard.

After a time, the horrible noises ended. "Wait here," Catherine said, then, despite my protests, went downstairs alone. My family and I waited in the upstairs parlor, straining our ears. All that we could hear was the lady's gentle, soothing voice and the sound of soft sobbing.

Minutes later, Catherine reappeared. Her gown was stained crimson with blood. Quietly, she avoided our questions and went to an iron safe in her husband's study. She opened the safe and withdrew a small bag of gold coins and a folded document. "Come with me," she said, and the four of us went down to the ground floor of the Fontenot house.

The marble floor was splattered with streaks of fresh blood, leading from the darkness of the courtyard beyond. "Stay here for a moment," Catherine requested. Her voice was rock steady, despite the carnage around her. As she slipped through the door of the downstairs sitting room, I caught a fleeting glimpse of huddled forms in the golden glow of a kerosene lamp. They were the forms of monsters—hideous fiends clad in blood-dyed rags. As the door swung shut, I watched as one of them looked my way, its eyes running the gamut from crimson to pink to eggshell white.

It was a demon I knew. A demon that possessed a familiar face, as well as a familiar voice. "Oh, what shame," it moaned tearfully. "What sordid shame!"

A moment later, Lady Catherine exited the study. She handed me the gold sack and the folded paper. "Here is money and your freedom. Take a buggy and two strong horses from the stable and go. Never return to this house again, and for God's sake, never utter a word of what took place here this night."

Confused, we did as she said. We left the house and stood for a long and horrified instant in the courtyard beyond the alabaster columns of the mansion. In the pale glow of moonlight we laid eyes on the massacre that the Fontenots' secret shame had brought about. Soldiers and horses lay everywhere, torn and broken, like huge toys mangled by some vicious giant-child and cast aside. Fresh blood glistened in the nocturnal light, as well as the stark whiteness of denuded bone. When I quickly led my family past the awful scene of human devastation, I noticed that some of the bodies appeared to have been partially devoured.

As we made our way through the garden for the stable, the titter of childish laughter erupted from beneath the spreading magnolia tree. "Jeremiah," called young Oliver from the shadows. "Come play with me."

My son took a step toward the tree, but I pulled him back. Moonlight shone upon the dirt circle where the child crouched. His marble game was different that night from the countless times I had witnessed before. For, instead of the colorful balls of glass, onyx, and agate, Oliver shot the circle with huge black orbs that seemed slick and slimy in appearance. It took me a moment before I realized that what he played with was the gouged eyes of a calvary soldier's horse.

We hitched two of the stable's finest steeds to a wagon and left that horrible place, escaping the Federal soldiers by way of a desolate backroad. Although I have never spoken of that horrible night before this writing, I have thought about it many times. I have revisited the Fontenot mansion many times in my dreams, have heard the bestial screams of bloodlust and smelled the coppery scent of violent death in my nostrils. And I always wake with a scream trapped firmly behind my lips. Sometimes that scream escapes, like steam escaping from a boiler, saving my mind from the mounting pressure of certain insanity.

I am an old man now. I have lived past the conquering of the West, past the turn of the century, and now into the time of the Great War. I have watched the world progress before my aged eyes, have seen people live and die, including my own family. And I have watched for word regarding a particular surname. That search has ended with a story from a recent newspaper, a report about a soldier by the name of Fontenot who was court-martialed for crimes unspeakable, even by the conventions of war. I cannot help but wonder if that poor soldier is a distant offspring of the family I once knew and if he is damned with the same seed of shame that his ancestors were.

I lay here now, bedridden and ill, my frail hands unfolding a document yellowed and crumbling with age. It is the declaration of freedom given to me some sixty years ago... my own private Emancipation Proclamation.

As I stare at the hastily scrawled signature at the bottom of the page, my heart grows heavy with uneasiness. For the name of Phillip Fontenot is signed not in simple ink, but in the blood of a dozen slaughtered souls.

THE WEB OF LA SANGUINAIRE

L arousse would not take him there at first.

"It not safe to travel de swamp at night," the old Cajun warned in his heavy French accent.

But Douglas Scott Price was accustomed to having his own way. An extra hundred dollars laid across the old man's leathery palm soon changed his tune.

The last rays of daylight played through the Spanish moss hanging from ancient cypress trees when the two climbed into Henri Larousse's pirogue, a canoe-like boat used by many of the trappers and fishermen in the area. "What's that for?" Price asked his guide when a double-barreled shotgun was laid across the center seat.

The elderly man shrugged. "De gators, dey would rather eat than sleep. Where we are going, dey be plenty of dem."

They began their long journey into the Louisiana bayou in silence. Price sat at the bow of the boat as Larousse rowed. Deeper into the swamp they drifted and deeper did the shadows gather, until the Coleman lantern next to the scattergun had to be lit. It cast an orange glow upon the two men. The lack of conversation was awkward, but they really had nothing to talk about. The only link between them was purely monetary.

A loon screamed off in the darkness, causing the young man to jump. The elder man chuckled softly and continued to row with slow, even strokes.

"So, what is it you do for a living?" the Cajun asked. Without conscious thought, he maneuvered the dugout across the dark waters, missing exposed roots and sandbars by mere inches.

"Oh, as little as possible, really," Price replied with an air of pomposity. "I was born into old family money. Ever heard of the New England Prices? No? Well, I expected as much. Being independently wealthy tends to mean a lot of free time, but I manage to keep myself busy."

Larousse had a good idea what sort of luxuries occupied Doug Price's time. Ferraris, eighty-foot yachts, and million-dollar thoroughbreds; a wet bar always at hand and a beautiful woman waiting at every point of the compass. Larousse knew his mind as well as he knew his own. Men of wealth and influence... you could almost smell the good fortune exude from them like the odor of some cheap cologne. The Cajun had been born in backwater poverty and had lived that meager life for nearly eighty years. He could sense a rich man a mile away, like a bluetick hound catching the scent of swamp coon upon a midnight breeze.

Seeing Larousse's amused eyes in the glow of the lamp, the young man continued. "Despite what you think, old man, I do not spend every waking hour jet-setting with a buxom blonde on my knee and a martini in my hand. No, actually my interests are quite respectable. My passion has always leaned toward the biological sciences, most particularly zoology. I've contributed millions to various zoological societies: the Smithsonian, the Audubon, the Sierra. I've also devoted much of my time. I've traveled the world over collecting rare species of bird, mammal, and insect life, both for public exhibition and for my own private collection."

"And so dat be de reason we are here, rowing through the bayou at such an ungodly hour?" asked the guide. "To collect something or other?"

"Yes," said Price, a little peeved. "But don't complain. You're being well paid for this little foray. In an hour or so, you'll be back at your humble swamp shanty, stuffing that three hundred inside your mattress. And I'll leave this godforsaken place with what I came here to find."

"And that would be de creature you mentioned before?"

"That's correct," said Price. "A rare species of the order Araneae. The pronunciation of its Latin nomenclature would likely be way over your head, old man, so I won't even bother. Needless to say, the common name of the arachnid is the striped swamp spider. It has a pale underbelly, the upper shell pitch black with broad streaks of crimson on the hind section. I do hope this isn't a wild goose chase you're taking me on. You are sure that you've seen such a spider in these parts?"

Larousse nodded. "Oui, a very large and ugly thing. But only at night... never in light of day."

"Yes, they are nocturnal in nature," agreed the collector. "And they are rather large—the size of a man's fist, or so I've heard. That is why I came prepared." He patted a ten-gallon aquarium at his feet.

The darkness grew thicker, the night sounds more varied, more mysterious to one unaccustomed to the swamps. They rounded a sharp bend between two waterlogged stands of old cypress and came upon a tangle of heavy cobwebs, stretching from one side of the channel to the other. Price directed the beam of a flashlight upon the vast webs, the glow etching each silver strand upon the darkness beyond. Fat-bodied spiders the size of golf balls scuttled away from the silken centers, away from the probing light.

"Hoo-boy!" exclaimed the Cajun. He watched the long-legged things climb swiftly upward into the obscurity of the dark limbs above. "Dere be you some spiders, Mr. Price. Plenty o' them. Oughta take a bucketful back with you."

The young man seemed disinterested. "Common water spiders." He tore away the fragile network of webs with a swing of his arm and they continued on. "They've been an item of my arachnid collection for years. It is the swamp spider I'm looking for now."

They moved on into the bayou, into far reaches where the boldest of poachers dared not come, even in broad daylight. The roar of a bull gator rumbled to their left, but it was too far away to present any immediate danger.

"De thing you seek... de swamp spider... it has an interesting history, it do," Larousse said. The glow of the kerosene lamp highlighted every little wrinkle, every line and liver spot on his aged face. "Some of de Cajun people, dey still believe in de old ways, de magic and de beliefs of dere ancestors. When de French first settled de bayou, dey believed in such things. De spider of which you search, dey called it *La Sanguinaire*, "The Bloodthirsty", for it was said to be big enough to catch and devour prey larger than other insects. Birds, rabbits, dere was even a case of one trapping a wild boar in its awesome web. Some, dey say, dat even a man would fall prey every now and again, and de Sanguinaire would crawl down out of de trees and drain him of his blood. Many thought, and still do, dat dey are de souls of de damned left upon earth as punishment, left as things repulsive to be loathed by man. Some think dat dey possess magical powers... dat if a man be bitten upon de crown of de head by a Sanguinaire, he is subject to dere very wishes for de remainder of his life... to watch over dem, to protect, to provide food, if it be necessary."

Douglas Price laughed out loud at the old man's story. "And do you, old timer..." he asked with a grin, "believe these stories of the Sanguinaire?"

"I do not so much believe or disbelieve, as I respect dem. Dere be many things, Mr. Price, that are unknown to us... many strange and awful things. If you are to travel in strange lands and deal with strange people, you would do well to learn to respect local customs and not scoff so easily."

"Enough of this mumbo jumbo," said Price. "Back to the business at hand." He flashed his light upon the trunks of the cypress trees along the heavy thicket that grew dense on the mossy banks. The wide swath of light swept the shallow bank to the right, then settled there. Movement came from the shadows between a clump of gnarled, exposed roots. "Take me over there! Quickly, man, before they get away!"

Larousse steered the pirogue to the far bank as his passenger prepared the glass tank. Price slipped on a pair of heavy rawhide gloves and, when they reached the tangle of roots, handed the flashlight to the old man. "Shine the light on that opening there," he indicated. The old man nodded sourly, thinking that the whole situation was somewhat ridiculous. All this fuss for a stupid spider! But he remembered the trio of hundred-dollar bills tucked in the pocket of his goose down vest and did as he was told.

The pale light revealed an entire nest of the spiders, great and bulky, glistening black with streaks the color of freshly-let blood crossing their hindquarters. They tried to escape into the webbed tunnels they had constructed beneath the shelter of the cypress roots, but Price quickly dispatched two of the larger ones, placing their writhing bodies into the aquarium and clamping on the screened lid.

"Good Lord!" breathed the young man, his face livid with excitement. "Will you look at the size of these things? They're three times larger than the common tarantula." The two swamp spiders clawed at the glass walls, fairly the size of full-grown tree squirrels.

The Cajun laughed, his broad grin showing off raw gums and a few tobacco-stained teeth. "Aw, I have seen much larger than those," he said, handing the flashlight back to its owner.

Price stared at the old gentleman, unable to determine whether the swamper was serious or just pulling his leg. He studied the two monstrous specimens in the glow of the Coleman, then glanced at his Rolex. It was a quarter after nine. "You get us back to town by midnight, old-timer, and I'll up your fee by another two hundred. Fair enough?"

Larousse nodded, his eyes hidden in the shadow of his oily fishing cap. "Oui, Monsieur Price. That would be most generous." He began to guide the low boat back into the channel from which they came.

For hours they traveled the labyrinth of channels that made up the still-water bayou. For some reason, the night sounds that had seemed so prominent before were now oddly absent. Price was aware of this, as well as the unfamiliarity of the swamp they now cruised, a swamp more densely overgrown than the one they had set into earlier in the evening. He wanted to mention the fact openly several times, but the elderly guide seemed so confident in his navigation that Price had let it go. *Probably just a shortcut back to the settlement,* he concluded. *For an extra two hundred, I bet the old geezer could find a shortcut clear to the gulf from here.*

Once, a curious gator crossed the dark waters and slammed his blunt snout against the side of the pirogue. The impact caused the lantern to topple off the center seat and over the side with a splash. When Price asked him why he hadn't fished it out, Larousse only smiled. "I can afford to lose a lantern. I have lost many to de swamp. But I can't afford to lose an arm. Look."

Price understood when he directed his flash upon the channel and saw half-a-dozen hungry gators floating like logs to either side of the boat.

They moved onward down the winding channel. The young collector was gradually aware that the darkness around them had thickened. The full moon that had hung overhead was gone, obscured by overlapping branches, heavy mats of Spanish moss... and something else.

He directed his beam ahead of them. A velvet wall of light mist choked the inlet a few yards ahead. "Looks as though a fog has rolled in," he said, gathering his jacket closer around him.

"Oui," replied the Cajun. "De fog... it gets as thick as gumbo in de bayou. So thick, in fact, that you can reach out and grab a fistful of it, if you so wish." His passenger shook his head skeptically at the old man's tale. "Really, monsieur. Go ahead and give it a try."

They were upon a wall of white mist now and, just to show the old man how idiotic his idea was, Price thrust his hand over the bow. His smug expression melted into confusion as his hand sank into something unsolid, yet of definite substance. It was sticky and clinging and, when he attempted to pull his hand away, found that he could not.

"Something has a hold of me, old man," he gasped. He batted at the adhesive strands with the aluminum flashlight, but it too became entangled. It dangled in the silky wall, despite its weight. "Help me, Larousse! Dammit, man, get me out of this confounded mess!"

Then he felt the distinct sensation of the boat sliding out from underneath him and realized that it actually was. With a curse, he lost his balance as he attempted to stand up and his entire weight lurched backward into the wall of unyielding mist. He was overcome with sudden terror when he realized that his body was now suspended over the dark water. He craned his head around and saw Larousse rowing the pirogue away from him, maneuvering to head back the way they had come.

He watched as Henri Larousse began to row back up the channel. The flashlight bobbed crazily in its suspension, throwing light upon the retreating boat.

Larousse totally ignored Price's pleas for help. He didn't even turn around. He absently removed his cap to scratch his balding head.

The shimmering glow of the battery-generated light revealed two deep indentations on the back of the old man's skull. Two ugly marks that seemed to sink clear past the bone to the brain, yet that had healed over many years ago.

Douglas Scott Price screamed loudly and fought furiously with the spiral of viscid silk that imprisoned him. But, of course, there was no escape. As the darkness swallowed the old Cajun and his boat, Price was keenly aware of movement in the trees above. When he finally saw the things creeping down the web toward him, as big as pit bull terriers, his mind snapped and he began to shriek madly.

"Bon Appetite," called Old Larousse from out of the night.

But the young man was beyond hearing him. Only the Sanguinaire acknowledged his well wishes, before they resumed their feeding.

N'AWLINS HAUNTED CRYPT TOUR

Mike McCullagh made his way from telephone pole to telephone pole… to store windows to the front of soda machines, and on to bus stop benches. He pulled a collapsible wagon, the kind you buy at Walmart or Costco. Its bed was half full of advertisements printed on ghostly blue paper. As he went from one intended point to another, the elderly man with the bushy gray beard juggled a staplegun and a tape dispenser, looking over his shoulder the entire time.

True, it was 3:30 AM and there was hardly anyone on the streets of New Orleans, and what he was doing wasn't unethical—technically illegal, yes—but nothing that really hurt anyone. Even still, he wore black sweatpants, a black hoodie, and sunglasses, which made it difficult to see in the dark. He didn't want to be recognized, though, in case one of NO's finest cruised by and caught him in the act.

He jumped at the sound of someone snoring and looked over to see a man slumped in the shadows of a doorway, fast asleep. One of the city's increasing population of homeless. *You'll end up like that, or worse, if something doesn't change… and soon,* he thought to himself.

He left State Street Drive, crossed Earhart Boulevard into Gert Town, and started down the sidewalk to Audubon Street. He paused at a phone pole, slapped a sheet of paper against the curved wood, and stapled it into place with four loud *pops*. Mike stepped back a few feet and was annoyed to discover that it was upside down. He considered ripping it off and putting up another. *Who's gonna give a shit?* he thought. Then, shucking off the shades so he could see what he was actually doing, he rushed to the front of a Starbucks and taped a flyer to the front door.

A streetlight illuminated the sheet of paper and he nodded with approval.

MORTICIAN MIKE'S
N'AWLINS HAUNTED CRYPT TOUR!
SEE WHERE THE GHOSTS DWELL !
RIDE IN A REAL HEARSE!
LAFAYETTE—METAIRIE—SAINT LOUIS CEMETERY

Let's see if she can top this after I wallpaper most of the Big Easy! he thought slyly. Then he set off with the wagon to finish his early morning mission.

Four hours later, Mike was sitting at the counter of a coffee shop called Beignets and Brews, when someone slid onto the stool next to him.

"You know if they catch you defacing city property, they're going to make you take them down. All of them."

Mike grunted, downed the dregs of his cup, and called for a refill. "My dear, that's what was once called advertising. The oldest and purest form of the practice. Perfected by medicine show barkers and freak show carnivals. Good ol' paper placards and word of mouth."

He looked over at the woman sitting next to him. She was tall and willowy, and forty years his junior. Long black hair in a Bettie Page cut, face the color of creamed coffee, and lips as red as freshly-let blood. She was dressed in tight black leggings, a white silk blouse with oversized bowtie, and a black, waist-length coat that was half circus ringleader and half funeral shroud. The thing that irked Mike the most was the thing on her head. A tall, black top hat with sparkly purple lace for a hatband and a real, honest-to-goodness taxidermied bat perched on the front of the brim, its tiny fangs bared menacingly.

Put them all together and you had his main competitor. The one who ground broken glass into his shattered ego, despite her sunny disposition. The harbinger of chaos and financial ruin... at least in his case. His cheerful, fresh-faced nemesis, the mysterious Miss Wysteria.

"Those were the days, weren't they, Mike?" she said. She paid for a double caramel Frappuccino and took a long sip. "But times change. You've got to set the bar higher... explore all the options. That's where the money is."

"Yes," said Mike sourly. "Your damn high bar. TV spots, viral TikTok videos, and a fleet of antique funeral wagons with teams of white horses. And those seven electronic billboard spots around New Orleans, flashing your pretty face every thirty-three-point-five seconds."

Wysteria's painted brows lifted in surprise. "You've actually timed them?" She reached out with a black-nailed hand and laid it sympathetically atop his. "You really are angsting over this, aren't you?"

"Why shouldn't I?" the old man muttered. "You're running me out of business. How the hell am I supposed to compete with Wysteria's Old Orleans Vampire Excursion? An elegant wagon ride through the city's cemeteries with red wine and hors d'oeuvres, and hair-raising tales of the dreaded Nosferatu? Everything Dracula, Lestat, and *Salem's Lot* rolled into one frightful package... ending with a Mardi Gras-style celebration at midnight at the hallowed crypt of Anne Rice in Metairie." He glared at her resentfully. "And if that isn't bad enough, you stole my hat."

The young woman laughed and ran a finger lovingly along the brim. "Haven't you heard? Imitation is the greatest form of flattery. My success at this profession is all due to my hero, the OG of haunted graveyard tours, Mortician Mike!"

"Right." Mike laughed bitterly. "Your illustrious hero... the one you're slowly putting out to pasture. Making my brand of theatrics and entertainment seem dull and obsolete."

"Aw, stop it! Everyone loves the N'awlins Haunted Crypt Tour!" she said excitedly. "It was my favorite thing in the whole city...hell, the entire *world*... when I was twelve. Back when I was little Julia Tisdell. That's why I've devoted my life to this gig. It's all because of *you*."

"Remind me to wash my hair with gasoline and stick my head in the oven when I get home," he said. Mike called for another coffee, wishing it was a stiff shot of bourbon whiskey instead.

"All you need to do is roll with the times," she urged with a smile. "Update the Haunted Crypt Tour. Maybe rewrite your script, visit some out-of-the-way haunts, and breathe some fresh life into that tired, old spiel of yours. Junking that fossil of a Cadillac hearse would be a good start. You've been it driving since, when, 1982?"

1978, he thought, but didn't tell her that. "Truthfully, I've been thinking about tricking it out... turning it into a stretch hearse to hold more customers."

"There you go!" Wysteria said excitedly. "You have been thinking outside the box! Oh, and it's *guests*, Mike. They like to be called guests."

She sipped on her drink. "So, when are you planning to do it?"

"You think I actually have the money? Hell, I can't even pay the rent. You're siphoning every bit of the tourist trade away from me. You've got more business savvy, more capital, and, on top of that, freaking vampires!"

"Vampires are where it's at now," said Wysteria with a shrug. "I can't help that the out-of-towners are more allured to bloodsuckers than lost and sorrowful souls."

"So, if I changed my tour to Mortician Mike's N'awlins Haunted Vampire Tour…?"

"I'd sue your ass off," she said solemnly. She held her frown of distaste for a long moment, then burst out laughing. "Lighten up, Mike! Really, if things don't work out, you've always got a spot as one of my drivers. You can handle a team of horses, can't you?"

"I'm allergic to horses!" Angrily, Mike McCullagh hopped off his stool and started for the door. Before he left, he turned and snapped "Oh, and Wisteria is spelled with an I, not a Y."

"Y is more dramatic and mysterious," the girl in the top hat said. "Just like me. I'm here to stay, Mike. No need to blame me for your misfortune and loss of clientele. If the Haunted Crypt Tour can't cut it anymore, maybe you should consider retiring."

Never! Mike thought as he headed for home a couple of miles away. As a kid, Wysteria had been his biggest fan. As an adult, she was a pain in the ass and the one who was going to cause his forty-year career to crash and burn.

And he knew there was no way he was going to allow that to happen. Even if it took devious and desperate measures on his part to turn it all around.

That afternoon, Mike drove to the French Quarter.

He parked his two-toned, black-and-gray hearse in a narrow alleyway off Dauphine Street, then approached the entrance to a storefront of black brick and a single, plate-glass window displaying a variety of voodoo and black magic supplies. The sign overhead simply read VOODOO JACK'S—POTIONS & CHARMS.

He looked around, saw that no one was paying him any attention, and ducked inside. A bell jangled overhead, signaling his entrance. The interior was dark and cluttered, with shelves and aisles of bottled powders, dried herbs and roots, and other paraphernalia of the Dark Arts. On shelving in a dark corner there were dusty jars bearing what looked to be human organs—a heart, kidneys, spleen, a few he couldn't quite identify. There were also statuettes and totems of Papa Legba, Bondye, Maman Brigitte, and Baron Samedi, the Haitian god of death. On the wall, directly behind the cash register, was a portrait of Marie Laveau, the legendary voodoo queen of New Orleans.

An elderly black man with snow-white hair stepped from a back room. Curiously he eyed his potential customer. "May I help you?"

"Yes," said Mike. He ran his tongue nervously across dry lips, then came right out and said it. "I need something to settle a score."

Voodoo Jack nodded. "I may be able to assist you with such a task. I have a large selection of poisons and curse jujus to choose from." He nodded to a rack of voodoo dolls near the counter. "And, of course, there's always do-it-yourself."

"I don't particularly wish to kill anyone," Mike said. "Just incapacitate them for a long period of time."

Jack frowned. "In what way?"

"Paralysis. Do you have a potion or talisman that could do that?"

"I do. In both forms." The old man walked to the back wall and returned with a skull-headed locket on a silver chain. "Slip this around their neck and speak an incantation, and they will freeze in their tracks. Can't move a muscle or speak. They will still breathe and see… but will be trapped in the trance of the living dead."

"That should do," agreed Mike. He grinned inwardly. It would be satisfying to see his enemy completely speechless for a change, without that sweet, infectious smile on her lovely face. "How much?"

"Three hundred for the *gris-gris* and two hundred for the words to trigger the spell."

"But that's every cent I've got left in the world!" protested Mike.

"If you want it bad enough, it is a fair price," said Voodoo Jack. "Don't worry. I won't ask who you intend to paralyze or for what reason. That is your affair. Now, do you want it or not?"

Muttering beneath his breath, Mike McCullagh produced his wallet and shoved the money across the counter. Voodoo Jack pocketed the cash, took a pad and a pencil, and wrote down several words. He ripped the sheet from the pad and stuck it in the breast pocket of Mike's shirt, then studied the man's bearded face for a moment. "You seem familiar."

Mike's heart quickened. "Oh, I'm around. Here and there. Could've passed each other in the street or something."

The shop owner nodded. "You may be right."

Mike left the place and hurried to the alleyway where his hearse was parked. He looked down at the skull-headed amulet in his hand. Here's to new beginnings, he thought, then slipped the necklace into the pocket that held the incantation.

"I appreciate you meeting me out here this evening," Mike said. He was dressed in his Mortician Mike get-up: black tux, burgundy vest, and, of course, the top hat with various tarot cards stuck in the hatband. "I apologize for being such a horse's ass this morning. Must've got up on the wrong side of the bed."

Wysteria smiled warmly. "Oh, don't think anything of it. I'm just glad you called. I'm ready to help any way I can."

Earlier that afternoon, Mike had called the young woman and asked if she would show him some of the "out-of-the-way haunts" she had mentioned at the coffee shop. She had seemed delighted to hear from him and enthusiastic about assisting him in updating the Haunted Crypt Tour.

It almost made him feel lousy for what he was about to do.

Around five-thirty that evening, they found themselves in the furthest reaches of the old Saint Louis Cemetery. There, rows upon rows of ancient family crypts stood, their marble and granite walls streaked and stained black with mold and mildew. Many had been there since the early 1800s, long forgotten and in dismal disrepair. Several of the crypt doors stood open, either broken into by transients seeking shelter or local teenagers looking for a secluded spot to party and make out.

The two had driven there in Mike's hearse, then strolled among the catacombs for nearly an hour. Wysteria seemed well versed in the cemetery's history, pointing out several unique crypts and expounding on the families who had entombed their dead within them. Mike had jotted all she had said on a pad of paper, as though eager for the wealth of information she was giving him.

It was nearly seven o'clock when they reached a particularly desolate section of the cemetery. The sun was sinking low and deep shadows stretched between the rows of old mausoleums.

"How about one more before we go?" Mike asked. He indicated a tall marble vault with the name CORNWELL carved ornately over the open door. The sepulcher was stately and hinted of great wealth, with a winged angel standing watch on the peak of the roof. "This looks interesting. Shall we go in?"

Wysteria seemed doubtful. "It's getting pretty dark. I'm not sure we could see once we got inside."

"I brought a flashlight," said Mike. "Just in case." He took the flashlight from his pocket and snapped it on, then directed the circular beam inside.

The woman smiled and shrugged. "Okay. But this will have to be the last one." She checked the time on her cell phone. "It's almost showtime and my schedule is completely booked tonight."

"I promise," said Mike. "The very last one."

Together, they entered the crypt. It smelled wet and swampy. Several of the tomb lids had cracked and fallen apart, showing decayed caskets in the hollows within. The ceiling was heavy with old cobwebs and the walls were marred with graffiti from temporary occupants who didn't give a damn about history, tradition, or respecting the dead.

As Wysteria made her way toward the back of the mausoleum, Mike knew the time had come. He stumbled forward, bumping into the woman and knocking the hat from her head. "Oh, I'm terribly sorry!"

"No worries," she said, laughing. When she bent to retrieve the top hat, the old man acted. Swiftly, he slipped the skull-headed amulet over her head and around her neck. Wysteria seemed confused. "What are you—?"

In the glow of the flashlight, Mortician Mike fumbled with the slip of paper and read the incantation. Almost instantly, Wysteria's muscles began to stiffen and freeze, and a look of dawning terror seized her pretty face.

It was Mike's turn to laugh. He faced her and smiled sinisterly. "You really didn't think I would allow you to tear down all that I've built during the past four decades, did you?" he asked. "I'll not end up wandering the streets, eating out of dumpsters and sleeping on park benches, or, Heaven forbid, in dark, dank places like this. But you'll be here... if for only a while. Only long enough for me to get my business back up to par again. Then I'll come back and remove the curse. And neither of us will be the worse for my trickery."

The woman's frightened eyes told him that she didn't believe a word of his empty promise.

"Adieu, sweet Wysteria," Mike told her. Then, leaving her standing within the deepening darkness of the old crypt, he pushed the heavy iron door shut and locked it with a rusty skeleton key he had purchased at an antique shop on Royal Street.

Mike whistled cheerfully as he made his way through the maze of mausoleums to where his hearse was parked outside the vast iron gate of Saint Louis Cemetery. Then, with a sly smile on his bearded face, he left the lonely graveyard behind.

Days passed into weeks and weeks into months.

Gradually, Mortician Mike once again became the master of haunted tours in the grand, old city of New Orleans. As the Big Easy puzzled over the sudden disappearance of Miss Wysteria, he took full advantage of the situation. Before long, his nightly schedule—and his bank account—was so full that he quickly upgraded his business. Mike bought several stretch hearses and hired a full-time staff—a team of drivers well-versed in the ghost lore of the city's cemeteries and office help for marketing and scheduling nightly tours. He even bought spots on television and twelve electronic billboards on the freeway and other high-traffic areas in New Orleans.

And, with each lucrative night of sold-out tours, the one he had left in the obscure tomb of CORNWELL drifted further and further from his mind. Until, eventually, she was completely forgotten, as though she had never even existed.

Three months had nearly passed before Voodoo Jack finally found her.

The old man broke the lock with the help of a pry bar and wrestled with the weight of the vault-sized door. Sunlight squeezed past the gap, revealing the awful crime that had been committed.

Jack knelt next to the withered and decayed form of the woman, who had stood stone-still like a statue, until she had starved and eventually perished. Tears filled his aged eyes as he tenderly ran his fingers through her long, black hair.

"I am so very sorry, my dear, sweet Julia," he whispered. "I knew the man was up to no good when I sold him the juju, but I had no earthly idea that you were his intended victim!"

He stared into the face of the corpse, a face that had once been lovely and unblemished, but had been ravaged by the deterioration of death and eaten away, a little at a time by insects and rats. Jack wanted to look away, but he didn't. He looked upon the horror of what his granddaughter had become, letting it sear into the depths of his grieving mind.

Voodoo Jack took a leather bag and began to remove items and place them around her prone form. "True, I cannot return you to the beauty of body and soul that you once were, but you shall return nevertheless… to exact revenge upon the wicked man who did this to you!"

The old man sprinkled a fine, gray powder in a circle around Wysteria's lifeless body and lit six black candles. Then, taking an ancient book from the bag, he began to speak and pray to the voodoo gods of his elders.

Late the following afternoon, as Mortician Mike prepared for another lucrative evening, he walked out to his hearse and found a small slip of paper wedged beneath a windshield wiper.

It simply read: THE CRYPT IS EMPTY.

Mike's heart raced with mounting panic. He looked around, but saw no one who might have placed the note there.

Well, we'll just see about this! he told himself. Then he fired up the hearse's engine and headed west across town for Saint Louis Cemetery.

Traffic was heavy and it was nearly dark by the time he reached the necropolis. He parked his vehicle, then descended into the labyrinth of ancient granite and marble tombs.

When he reached the crypt of CORNWELL, he was shocked to find the door standing wide open. Mike breathed deeply and attempted to settle his nerves. He reached into his coat pocket and withdrew a snub-nosed revolver. If someone had discovered the body of the missing woman and intended to blackmail him, he intended to gun them down and leave them in the catacombs to rot.

Cautiously, he entered the shadowy interior of the crypt. At first, he saw nothing. The burial chamber looked to be completely empty. Then, from the shadows at the rear of the vault, movement caught his attention and he watched, mortified, as someone—or *something*—stepped into view.

It was a gaunt, skeletal form dressed in a moldy coat and stained silk shirt. It wore a familiar top hat upon its grizzled head, black with violet lace around the crown and a preserved bat perched upon the brim.

"Good Lord in Heaven!" cried Mortician Mike. "It can't be!"

"Oh, but it is I!" assured the corpse. Its vocal cords were as coarse and dry as rotten twine. "The one you condemned by your treacherous hand and left here to hopelessly await your return."

Mike stared in terror at the loathsome face of Wysteria. Her life's juices had dried up, leaving only sunken, withered flesh and exposed patches of stark, white bone. Rodents had fed upon her, stripping away the meat of her lips, nose, and ears, and he could see roaches and spiders skittering through her hair and the folds of her clothing.

And, in her bony hand, she held the skull-headed amulet on the silver chain.

"No!" he screamed, backing away.

"You cursed me with the living death!" Wysteria rasped. "Made me starve and suffer in this crypt!" Slowly, she shambled toward him. "Now it's *your* turn!"

"NO!" screamed Mike. "Stay away from me! Stay away!"

But, before he could turn to leave, Wysteria's left hand lashed out and closed around the column of his throat. Fingernails, jagged and long in death, burrowed into his flesh, refusing to let go. As Mike thrashed and squirmed, yearning for escape, the chain of the skull juju was slipped around his neck and the eldritch words were spoken.

Instantly, he grew silent and still. Deep within his chest his heart pounded wildly, but that was the only motion that he was allowed.

She's going to do the same to me as I did to her! his thoughts wailed. *She's going to lock me in this tomb, to waste away and die!*

Wysteria laughed coarsely. "I know what you are thinking, but that shall not be your destiny. You are deserving of something much more horrifying and lingering!" And, with that, she lifted the old man effortlessly in her arms and departed the open crypt.

The zombie carried him between the rows of silent mausoleums until they reached their intended destination. Mike was shocked to find one of Wysteria's finest, glass-paned funeral hearses waiting in the shadows. But the horses tethered to the wagon weren't snow white in color, but as black as Death itself.

Where are we going? he wondered as she opened the door at the rear of the wagon and gently deposited him in a rosewood casket that waited inside. *Where the hell is she taking me?*

"As I said before, true death will not befall you," she told him, as though reading his thoughts. "No, you shall endure the living death, condemned to the cellar of Voodoo Jack's shop. There, my grandfather shall slowly and meticulously harvest your flesh, bone, and organs for his various potions and *gris-gris*. It may take months, perhaps even years to completely use you up. During that time, you will not be able to move a muscle or utter a single scream, Mortician Mike. But you shall surely feel every moment of the terror and agony that will be slowly inflicted upon you!"

As the dread and shock of his predicament began to sink in, Mike heard Wysteria climb into the driver's seat and, with a flick of the reigns, begin to drive the funeral wagon across town, in darkness, toward his torturous fate.

SUCKERS!

Bertrand Pinet opened the letter from the New Orleans Coroner's Office, knowing very well that he would not like what he read.

He unfolded the sheet of paper, bypassed the medical jargon that seemed to be verbal overkill to his Acadian mind, and found the morsel of information that he was looking for. *The subject's cerebrum and cerebellum seem to have been forcefully removed, leaving the majority of the medulla oblongata intact. Liquefied remnants of the brain were evident in minute quantities within the cranial cavity. The source of the tissue's extraction was a 5.3-centimeter circular opening in the rear of the skull, located between the lambdoid suture and the posterior fontanelle.*

"Sweet Virgin Mary!" the sheriff of St. Adeline Parrish said softly in a thick Cajun accent. "We got some bad shit goin' on."

Almost immediately, his dispatcher and secretary poked her head through the door of his office. "You say something, Sheriff?"

"No, ma'am, Miss Lisette," he said, quickly slipping the letter beneath a stack of paperwork. "Nothin' to worry your pretty head over."

Lisette Dupree—seventy-two years of age, rail thin, with hair as black as a cottonmouth's back—eyed Bertrand suspiciously. "Do that letter pertain to those bodies found in the bayou?"

"Maybe…but that be official police business, Miss Lisette. Being as you're not a police lady, but in the administrative branch, you needn't concern yourself about it."

"Don't you be giving me that, Sheriff," she said haughtily. "I'm a tax-paying citizen here of St. Adeline, so's it *is* my business!" She frowned, her eyes bugging behind her horn-rimmed spectacles. "Folks being found dead, heads and bodies caved in, *empty*, some sucked dry of every last drop of blood…it is hellacious! You ask me, that doctor out yonder near Roubechoix Point is the one up to no good. Out there by his lonesome, doing God only knows what!"

"Now you go leaving Otis Louviere alone," Bertrand told her.

"He's a fine doctor and I got no reason of suspecting him of anything. Besides, he's a scientist doing wondrous things. Remember how he treated Aileen Chauvin's smallest girl? The one with the gimpy leg three inches too short? Louviere, he gave her shots and that leg grew right on out, pretty as you please. Miraculous!"

"Satan's balm is more like it! Louviere out there, thirty-eight years old, no wife, no young'uns, living in the boonies with his laboratory of potions. He's not to be trusted, that man."

"You are of a sour disposition this morning, Miss Lisette," said Bertrand wearily. "Leave the poor man be."

The old woman began to return to her desk. "Get the lead out of your toot-toot, Bertrand, and earn your dollar. Find out what—or *who*—is responsible for what is going on!"

That's what I be trying to do, he thought, disgruntled. *Meddling, old bitch -lady.*

Bertrand Pinet looked at the coroner's letter peeking out from beneath the papers and considered taking the crime photos from his bottom drawer--photos of sunken bodies, drained of fluids and organs snapped by a digital camera he had purchased at the Walmart in Baton Rouge. He thought better of it, though. If Lisette caught sight of those pictures, she would be out in the middle of the street like a brass band, telling everyone within earshot.

With a groan of effort, he left his chair and walked outside. As he was climbing into his jeep, a voice crackled over the radio. It was his deputy, Armand Fruge.

"I out here south o' town, Sheriff...at Clovis Thibodaux's pier. We got us another one and fresh!"

Bertrand shook his head and turned his key in the starter. "Hold on...I'm a-coming."

Sheriff Pinet was headed down the boardwalk of the pier, when he saw his deputy and Clovis Thibodeaux standing at the end, looking down into the water.

Clovis was old—hell, he was old when Bertrand was born thirty-six years ago—and made his livelihood trapping and fishing, or so he claimed. The elderly man was thin as an eel and mean as a gar, and if he bathed, no one had ever laid witness to it. He wore the only set of clothes anyone had ever seen him in: an oily baseball cap, flannel shirt, faded overalls, and knee-length waders. His constant companion, a mange-ridden bluetick hound named Pierre, lay next to him with his head on his paws and his tail drumming the boards.

"Where is he?" Bertrand asked his deputy.

"In the water, among the pilings," Armand told him. "But it be a *she*, not a he."

Bertrand walked up to the edge of the pier and looked down. A skinny woman with stringy brown hair with cherry-red highlights floated in the murky water. Her tattooed arms were pale blue and slightly bloated, and she was dressed in an orange tank top and cut-off denim shorts. One foot still wore a green rubber flip-flop, while the other was bare and pruny.

"Let's get her out," the sheriff instructed. The three of them got down on hands and knees and lifted the corpse from the water. Despite the fact that it was water-logged, the body seemed surprisingly light.

Gently, they turned her over and laid her out on the boards of the pier.

"Well, I'll be damned," said Bertrand. "Rosella Rivette." He grimaced. His wife, Zenobia, would be mighty upset. Rosella had been her best friend in high school. They'd gotten their first tattoos together, at Gustave's House of Ink.

"Didn't she serve eighteen months for meth possession?" asked Deputy Fruge.

"Twelve," the sheriff clarified. "Another six for prostitution."

"The gal had a rough life, she did," Clovis told them. "Her papa, he lavished more affection on her than was proper."

Bertrand looked at him. "Jacked the springs with her, did you?"

The old man shrugged his narrow shoulders. "A couple of times or three, I suppose."

They stared at the woman's face. It was sunken in, the same way Wayne Mazerolle's head had after the brains had been sucked out of the back of his skull, according to the autopsy report.

"Well, she ain't gonna get no dates now, for damn sure," said Armand.

The sheriff knelt and laid a hand on her stomach. The flesh was flaccid, the abdomen hollow underneath. The pressure of his hand caused the corpse to release a loud, wet fart that was both comical and nauseating at the same time. Nasty black water shot from the frayed legs of her shorts, pooling on the boards.

"Get back, gents," warned Clovis. "Watch your shoes!"

Bertrand studied the body for a long moment, then took a Case pocketknife and folded out the sharpest blade. He pushed back her head with the toe of his boot and jabbed the steel into her carotid artery.

"Shit!" declared Thibodaux. "What you gone and done?"

"Just testing a theory." And the lawman's hunch proved right. No blood was in the artery at all. Rosella Rivette had been bled completely dry.

"What would do that to someone?" the deputy wondered.

Clovis's ancient eyes peered off across the swamp. "I'm thinking I be knowing."

"What then?"

"Been seeing some frightful things out yonder," he told the two. "Peculiar things whilst I've been out fishing."

"You mean poaching," Bertrand clarified.

"Naw, naw...fishing."

"More like poaching," the sheriff said once again. "Gator...maybe out of season?"

"Catfish," the old man insisted. "A snapping turtle or two." He glared at Bertrand. "You want to contradict or listen to what I be saying to you?"

The sheriff backed off a bit. "Go on."

A spooked look shown in the elderly man's eyes. "As I be saying, seen some mighty queer things out there. Ticks as big as softballs and skeeters the size of Ol' Pierre there, with wings five feet across. Flying through the evening sky in formation, like a flock of gooses, they were."

"You certain you weren't drinking that old kick-ass shine you like to brew?" asked Bert. "Maybe you seen them giant swamp spiders, too. *La Sanguinaire*?"

"I ain't lying, Sheriff! I seen them things with my own twin eyes!" Clovis looked as if he'd had his feelings hurt. "You don't be thinking much of me, do you, Pinet?"

"Can't say as I do. But go on."

Clovis cleared his throat and continued. "Found some critters on the banks of the bayou and on the sandbars...rabbits, coons, a white-tail deer...hollowed out like an empty sack. Touched 'em with a stick and their bones just gave way, collapsed. One critter...a good-sized possum...had something living inside it. Thrashed around, twisting and turning, like a snake, but it weren't none. Didn't prod it to see, neither. Afraid I was, that it would slither out and grab hold of me!"

"Still sounds like a gallon drunk of skull-bust, in my opinion," Bertrand said skeptically. "Any idea where these things came from?"

"Not sure about the ticks or the thing in the possum, but the skeeters, they be flying from the direction of Roubechoix Point."

Armand's eyes widened. "That there crazy doctor! Louviere!"

The sheriff looked irritated at his deputy. "Not you, too."

"It be true!" said Clovis. "I swear to it on my Mee-ma's grave, bless her soul. It was Otis Louviere's house that they flown from."

"Everybody gotta have them a scapegoat," said Bertrand, shaking his head. He looked down at the whore's body. "I'm going to the jeep to call Mr. Dubois to bring his hearse. I suppose we be sending poor Rosetta to the morgue in N'awlins, as well."

"If'n they have enough tables and drawers left by now," said Clovis, eyeing the sunken woman with distaste.

That night, Bertrand and his wife sat at the kitchen table, sharing a bottle of Pernod Ricard, most of which his woman had downed. Zenobia had wept tears over Rosetta, for they had been inseparable up until graduation, when they had parted for their separate paths in life.

"She was a good 'un, Rose was," Zee sobbed, taking another swallow from a jelly jar glass with Scooby Doo on the front. "She was wild and couldn't keep her legs together ten minutes, but she had herself a good heart, she did."

Bertrand took the bottle and capped it. "That enough for you tonight," he told her. "You know liquor gives you the runs. Best leave it alone."

"Look in on the babies, will you, Bertrand?" she asked, leaving the kitchen and dropping dizzily onto the cushions of the living room couch. "I think I'm in no condition to play mommy. My head is swimming like a seasick catfish."

Bertrand nodded and left her there. He walked down the narrow hallway to the children's room at the far end of the house. The bedroom light was off, but a small nightlight glowed from an outlet near the closet. He could barely see his daughter, Ophelia, in her toddler bed and his infant son, Philippe, in his crib. Bertrand crossed the floor in his sock feet, kissed them both on the forehead, then crouched down and scratched their mutt-dog, Gambit, behind its floppy ears. Satisfied, he left the room and started back to the living room, certain that Zee would likely be stretched out on the couch and sound asleep.

He was nearly there, when he heard a dry rasping sound behind him. He turned just in time to see something long and pale slither into the children's bedroom.

His heart hammered in his chest. *What the hell was that?* he thought. He stood there, frozen in his tracks, listening for the sound of Gambit growling or barking. The dog did neither. *That be odd. Ol' Gambit wouldn't let a housefly get ten feet from the young'uns without pitching a fit.*

Bertrand walked to the hall closet, opened it silently, and took his service revolver from the gun belt hanging on a peg inside. He checked the loads. Five in the chambers, one empty beneath the hammer. Slowly, he walked down the hallway and peeked through the open door.

All seemed as it had before, but he knew that was a lie. Something had entered the room. A snake? The thought coated his heart with ice. He cocked the gun, turning the cylinder, and bringing a round into line. Cautiously, he stepped inside, holding the .38 pistol ahead of him.

It was a moment before he realized that all was not as he had left it. The floor of the bedroom between the bed and crib was empty. Gambit was nowhere to be seen.

Step by step, he traveled the length of the room, looking from left to right. The palm of his hand grew slick with sweat, making the walnut grips of the Smith & Wesson difficult to hold. *Come on, Gambit, boy. This is not like you. Did you find that ol' viper and make a midnight snack of him?*

He was nearly to the bedroom window, when he heard the sound of something gasping for breath...or, rather, strangling for breath. It came from the far side of his daughter's bed, near the closet. Carefully, he stepped around the whitewashed footboard, until he could see what was happening in the glow of the nightlight.

Gambit lay on the floor entwined by a constricting length of twisted white muscle. It wasn't a snake, though; not a swamp snake nor a boa or python. This thing was nearly six feet long and strangely flat...not round and thick like a serpent. He watched in terror as the thing slowly and methodically forced its way through Gambit's open mouth and down his throat into the depths of his bowels. The dog was dying; he could see the glassy look in the canine's dark brown eyes.

What is it? he thought wildly. *Oh, dear God, it looks like... like a...*

Bertrand knew that firing his gun was out of the question. He laid the revolver on a toy box nearby and quietly raised the bedroom window. Gathering his nerve, he bent and grabbed the convoluted mixture of dog and writhing monster, intending on carrying it to the open window and tossing it out.

That was when dear, sweet Ophelia woke up and sat straight up in bed. She scrubbed the sleep from her eyes. "Daddy?" asked the girl. Then, seeing what was in his hands, she began to scream.

A moment later, Zee had snapped on the bedroom light. Stunned, she stood in the doorway, her face pale and her eyes as wide as saucers. "Bertrand! What is that thing?"

The sheriff said nothing at first. Then he stared at the ugly thing in his hands, squirming and thrashing as it made its way, inch by torturous inch, down the little dog's throat. "Lord help us all, Zee...I do believe it is...a *tapeworm!*"

Then he stepped to the window and flung it far off into the darkness of the Louisiana night.

Soon, Zee had grabbed their daughter, while Bert held his crying son close to his chest. Together, they stood at the window. The light cast its glow upon the dewy grass of the yard outside. They caught a glimpse of pale motion as the long, flat creature slithered toward the thicket that bordered the edge of the Pinet property, dragging the motionless carcass of the dog behind it.

Holding the squalling Philippe in the crook of one arm, he reached down with the other and took the gun off the top of the toy box. "Grab the diaper bag," he told Zee. "I'm taking you to your mama's."

"Where you be going then?" she asked, wild with fear.

"To find out what's happening here in St. Adeline Parrish," he told her. "And I do believe I know where to go about finding the answer."

It was nearly midnight when Bertrand Pinet parked his jeep by the highway. Taking a twelve-gauge shotgun from the back seat, he slowly made his way across the marshy earth that bordered the dark water-way of Roubechoix Point.

Before leaving the house, he had called Armand and told him to round up Clovis Thibodaux, his johnboat, and every gun they could gather, and meet him at the dock behind the old Louviere house. After finding four organ-ravaged and exsanguinated bodies during the past two weeks—as well as the monstrous tapeworm that had killed poor Gambit—the Cajun lawman knew that they had no time to waste. The threat had to be identified and eliminated, more by force than by due process of law.

The old, two-story plantation house had once been the heart of a sugar plantation owned by the Louviere family back in the mid-1800s—a majestic palace built of money and power, immaculately white and surrounded by tall cypress trees laced with long beards of Spanish moss. But now, nearly a hundred and seventy years later, it was simply a deteriorating remnant of the Old South and its forgotten days of glory and prosperity.

Bertrand cautiously traveled down a worn path through a dense thicket of high thistle and blackberry bramble. Up ahead, the old house—scrubbed bare of its white paint by decades of harsh weather and humidity—loomed before him. All the windows were dark, like the empty sockets of a skull, except for a single one on the ground floor, which glowed brightly, casting a long slice of yellow light across the trail of moss and black earth.

He was halfway to the old mansion when he heard the singing of crickets cease. Bertrand stood, frozen, in the silence for a long moment, then heard a peculiar noise echo from the direction of the bayou. He peered into the darkness but could see nothing over the tall brush. Then the noise—a shrill, high-pitched *buzzing*—seemed to lift skyward and head straight toward him.

The sheriff looked toward the pale orb of a full moon. His heart leapt in his chest when he saw several dark forms silhouetted in its glow. He considered turning and running back to the jeep, but it was too late. The squadron of airborne monstrosities was suddenly descending upon him.

They were mosquitoes...giant ones. He remembered Clovis telling him of skeeters as big as Ol' Pierre the coonhound with wings five feet across. These were much larger: about the size of a year-old calf with a wingspan of six and a half feet or more. Even in the gloom, he could see that the body and legs of the pest alternated in bold stripes of black and white, identifying it as a tiger mosquito, a species common in the area's bayous and deltas. Bertrand recalled jokes that had been going around for years, such as how the mosquito was the state bird of Louisiana. Looking at the things that swooped toward him, that wisecrack seemed more accurate and less humorous than it had before.

He lifted his pump shotgun and fired, peppering one with double-aught buckshot. The skeeter crumpled in mid-air and dropped to the marshy earth. He dispatched a couple more, then heard buzzing coming up fast from behind. He whirled to fire, but a giant skeeter dropped low and knocked him bodily off his feet. The twelve-gauge went spinning off into the thicket. Bertrand found himself lying on his back in the damp earth, staring up at six of the winged creatures hovering directly overhead.

He shucked his .38 revolver from its holster, just as one of the things dropped and lit on his right leg. One of its suckers—long and firm and as thick as a garden hose, punched through the denim of his jeans and burrowed into the meat of his thigh, searching for an artery to drain. He screamed at the pain and fired twice at the thing, missing once, before striking it in its limber body. The skeeter shrieked with an ear-piercing, insectile cry and flew off, dragging its sucker out of Bertrand's leg. He felt warm blood soak his pants leg from the ugly hole in his thigh.

The scent of blood seemed to drive the hovering group of mosquitoes wild. They dipped and dived, their dark eyes gleaming hungrily at him. There were five of them and only three rounds left in his gun. He fired at one, but his target bobbed and weaved, dodging the shot. Bertrand was certain they would drop, en masse, and completely drain him of his blood, when a loud report cracked through the night…a rifle shot. One of the winged monsters veered sharply and slammed into the trunk of a cypress tree, dead before it hit. A volley of gunshots rang out and the others fell about him in loud thuds, bony legs kicking and wings fluttering until they grew still in death.

"You okay, Sheriff?" asked Armand Fruge, running from the direction of the dock. Clovis followed closely behind, holding a Winchester rifle in his wrinkled hands. "Damn! You been shot?"

"Naw, one of them giant skeeters lit on me and sunk its sucker into the meat of my leg," Bertrand told him. "Hurts like hell, but it ain't bleeding near as bad as it was before." With some effort, he got up and limped toward the big house. "I'm going to find out what's going on. Ain't natural, what I've been seeing tonight."

Clovis kicked at one of the fallen skeeters. It was as limp and light as an empty trash bag. "Hooo boy! Don't that be the honest truth."

Soon, they were on the front porch and banging on the big double doors of ornately-carved oak. No one answered at first, then they heard the sound of a deadbolt disengaging and one of the doors swung open. A pudgy, middle-aged man wearing thick-lensed glasses and a lab coat stood there. He held a 9mm pistol in one hand and his face was blanched and pale with fear.

"Quickly!" he hissed, his magnified eyes looking warily into the dark sky overhead. "Come inside!"

Once they were in the spacious foyer of the plantation house, Otis Louviere locked and bolted the door securely. He looked at the gun in his hand and self-consciously crammed it into a pocket of his lab coat. "So, what brings you here at this time of night, gentlemen?"

"What in blue blazes have you been doing up here, Louviere?" demanded the sheriff.

"Making himself some big-ass monsters!" accused Clovis, eyeing the doctor with contempt.

Louviere raised his hands in defense. "Not intentionally. Things… well, they've sort of gotten a little out of hand."

"A *little*?" declared Armand. "Four innocent folk dead, they innards sucked out, and the sheriff here with a hole in his leg big enough to drive a Buick through!"

"Come into my laboratory," he told them. "I will fix up Bertrand's leg and tell you what's happening."

Soon, the doctor was administering first aid and telling his story. "For several years I have been experimenting with growth hormones, hoping to develop a strain strong and stable enough to cure such physical anomalies as dwarfism and birth defects. I have had some success with several children here in the parish, but the strain was too weak to effectively treat adults. So, I launched a new series of tests and increased the strength to a much greater potency. Initially, I used small animals as my test subjects: squirrels, rabbits, possums. But the strain seemed to be more than they could handle, and they died within hours. So, I lessened the potency and tried other subjects. Parasitic insects and worms seemed to absorb and sustain the hormone best. There were plenty of species to be found here in the swamp. But halfway through my tests, something went wrong. Their metabolisms and their rate of absorbing and processing the hormone caused them to grow to gigantic proportions. The bigger they became, the more aggressive they grew. I tried to contain them, but I returned to the lab one morning to find that they had escaped…into the swamp."

"What all did you experiment on?" Clovis asked him.

"Common varieties of parasitic organisms indigenous to our area," Louviere told him. "Mosquitoes, ticks…"

"Tapeworms," added Bertrand.

The doctor's eyes enlarged behind the lenses of his glasses. "So, you found it?"

The sheriff nodded. "It found me…or, rather, my dog. Killed it. Crushed it like a boa constrictor and forced its way down its throat."

"Alas, poor Pierre, he is dead, too," said Clovis. He glared hatefully at the doctor. "Earlier tonight, something, it latched onto his side and sucked his guts clean out. Nothing left but an empty sack of bones and hide."

Armand removed his hat solemnly. "Poor Gambit and Pierre! Gone to that great coon hunt in the sky."

The old man wiped his eyes with a filthy bandana. "A beautiful sentiment! Thank you, Deputy."

When the doctor had finished working on Bertrand's leg, the lawman limped to one of the laboratory windows and looked out. "So, what can we do to fix this problem, Doctor?"

Louviere's face grew as pale as lard. "Our only course of action would be to venture into the swamp and destroy the test subjects. I would prefer to capture them alive for further study, but they have grown much too aggressive and too dangerous."

"And, after they are destroyed, you will discontinue your experiments," emphasized the sheriff.

"Yes," said the scientist. "What about the people who were killed?"

"I reckon you'll be brought up on manslaughter charges...for bringing about their deaths. I'm sorry but I don't see any way to avoid that."

Otis Louviere nodded. "I suppose that is a fair price to pay for my stupidity."

Bertrand looked at the men around him, seeing the grim expressions in their eyes. "Okay, then it's settled. Let's get it done."

They left by the mansion's rear door and headed through the darkness in the direction of the bayou. Clovis Thibodaux's johnboat was tied there, waiting for their dreaded excursion into the dark depths of the swamp.

The four climbed into the boat, silently watching for menacing movement in the night. Clovis disengaged the rope that was tethered to the dock and, starting the engine, sent them slowly down the channel, toward the heart of the bayou. The old man clicked on a spotlight. It cast a swath of pale illumination upon the dark waters and the gnarled cypress trees that stood to either side, their limbs bowing low and dangling thick with Spanish moss.

For a while, all they saw were gators lying on the mossy banks and a few snakes resting on rocks and low-hanging branches, maybe a gar or a barnacle-crusted snapper. Then, the further into the swamp they traveled, those familiar life forms dwindled, almost as though becoming extinct. Even the night birds and insects were silent, if they were even there at all.

The boat was moving beneath a particularly dense canopy of moss-laden branches, when something began falling out of the trees.

At first, Bertrand thought they were brown pie plates, although the idea seemed downright ludicrous. Then one of the flat objects fell across his back and scuttled sluggishly up the nape of his neck, heading for the rear of his skull. He knew then exactly what it was. "Ticks!" he yelled. Reaching around, he grabbed the parasite and flung it away. It landed in the dark water of the channel with a loud splash.

Clovis and Louviere fought with the things as they caught hold and hung onto their clothing. Then, behind him, Armand Fruge began to scream.

The old man directed the light toward the rear of the johnboat. The deputy was covered with them. The giant ticks had bitten deep and dug in, sucking hungrily at his head, chest, back, and belly. There was even one hanging from the junction of his groin. As he dropped to the floor of the boat, Bertrand and Louviere rushed to his side.

"Get us the hell outta here!" the sheriff ordered. Clovis did as he was told and, soon, they were away from the tick-infested branches, into open water.

Armand was flailing and hollering in agony. "It hurts, oh dear Jesus!" he hollered. "The pressure! I can't stand it!"

"What can we do?" asked the sheriff.

Louviere regarded the poacher. "Do you have a knife? Two if you have them?"

Clovis drew a long-bladed knife with a wicked point from a sheath on his hip and handed it to the doctor. He found a curved skinner in a compartment near the boat's dash and gave it to the sheriff.

"The heads are anchored deep," said Louviere. "We'll have to carve them out. But we'll need to do it quickly." He pointed to several of the monstrous ticks. Their flat bodies were beginning to swell, filling with fluid and tissue.

They went to work on Armand's head first. It took some doing, but they finally disengaged the tick's mandibles from the back of the deputy's skull. It left an ugly hole about the size of a quarter in the skin and bone. Bertrand removed his shirt and tied it around Armand's head, then went to work on another parasite. The man wailed and screamed as the knives whittled and carved, digging deep craters around the tick's stubborn heads. Finally, all were off. They heaved the ugly creatures over the sides of the boat, where they bobbed on the water like partially-inflated balloons. Louviere went to work, binding the deputy's wounds. They bled profusely and organs and tissue were even protruding from a few of the gaping bites.

"Turn this thing around, Clovis!" Bertrand ordered. "We gotta get Armand to the hospital!"

The metallic cocking of a hammer caused the two to turn around. Otis Louviere stood behind them, holding the 9mm steadily in his hand. "No," he said calmly. "We will be proceeding." He nodded to several wire cages Clovis had sitting in the bed of the boat. "And we will be bringing back as many specimens as possible." A small grin crossed his chubby jowls. "Or, rather, I will. You two gentlemen will receive a bullet for your troubles and will feed the gators, while I return to St. Adeline and continue my work."

"Treacherous son-of-a-bitch!" cussed Clovis. He looked at the Winchester leaning nearby but knew he would barely get three steps within reach before Louviere gunned him down.

"Proceed," the doctor insisted, his voice as cold as the blued steel in his fist.

Onward into the far reaches of the swamp they traveled. Each man was on the alert for fleeting motion or unusual sounds that would herald the presence of more parasites. But, for a half hour, there was nothing. The swamp seemed empty of wildlife.

Around three o'clock in the morning, Clovis slowed the boat to a halt and let the engine idle.

"Why did you stop?" asked Louviere.

"Something's in the water," the old man told him. He turned the spotlight on the churning currents ahead of the bow. Several long, glistening objects broke the surface, before sinking into the dark depths again.

"Gators?" asked Bertrand.

"No. Too soft and slimy. And too big."

The doctor motioned threateningly with his gun. "Remember, whatever we find goes back with me."

"These won't be fitting into no damned cage," Clovis said. He turned and looked at the man. Suddenly his ancient eyes widened in horror. "Sacré bleu!"

Puzzled, the doctor looked over his shoulder and his heart froze.

Something was rising up out of the dark waters behind the boat. It was black and glistening and impossibly large—tubular, like a worm, but much thicker. If it had eyes, Louviere could not see them. All he could see was its open maw ringed with hooked, shark-like teeth.

"It's..." Bertrand was at a loss for words at first, then found them as the thing lurched and swayed. "It's a *leech*!"

The creature emitted a guttural gurgling sound as it found its victim and lowered, much quicker than anyone expected for such a cumbersome organism. Louviere cried out, fired twice with his pistol, and then was swallowed—from the chest up—by the fanged mouth of the monstrous leech. Its teeth anchored deeply and its dark body began to pulsate as it sucked hungrily at its prey. Bertrand and Clovis could hear the doctor's muffled screams. His shrieks echoed within the gullet of the beast as his arms and legs jerked spasmodically.

It's sucking him clean out! thought the sheriff with horror. *Like I'd suck the innards from a boiled crawdad!*

Then, abruptly, the leech rose another seven feet into the muggy night air. The doctor's feet kicked wildly, dislodging a shoe, then the awful screaming stopped and he grew limp. With a loud splash and a gurgle, the monster descended back into the depths of the bayou, taking Otis Louviere's remains with it.

The sheriff and the poacher stood there for a long moment, watching and listening. The swamp was still around them and so was the water. Nary a ripple broke its mirror-like surface. Nothing else appeared... hungry, searching for sustenance.

At the back of the boat, Armand moaned, oblivious to what had just taken place.

"Let's get on back to town, Clovis," Bertrand suggested.

"Yes, sir," he agreed with a nod. "I be more'n ready to be rid of this dark place and the horrors that dwell here."

Clovis deftly turned the boat and started back up the channel. Above the bearded limbs of the cypress the night sky was like black velvet, studded with a million rhinestone stars.

Bertrand crouched next to his deputy. "We gonna get you some good help, Armand," he told him. "It's over."

"I think not, constable," said Clovis from the bow. "Look!"

Bertrand stood up. The old man was directing the beam of his spot along the banks of the bayou. Partially submerged in the still water and clinging to the exposed roots of the cypress trees were dark, waxy cylinders of some sort, narrow and pointed at the ends.

"What the hell is all that, Clovis?" he asked.

"Be looking like skeeter eggs to me," the poacher told him. The man's wrinkled face was pale and full of fright. "They be thousands of them!"

The sheriff thought for a minute. "Can we burn them?"

"I got me a two-gallon can of gasoline here, but that ain't gonna do much. We'll have to come back and get 'er done...and pray that they don't hatch before we do."

Bertrand Pinet shuddered. The thought of a massive, buzzing swarm of giant mosquitoes descending upon his hometown of St. Adeline Parrish was terrifying to even imagine. "Let's go then...and quick!"

Clovis nodded grimly and, pushing the johnboat's engine to the limit, they silently headed back up the dark channel of the bayou for home.

SATURDAY NIGHT AT MEE-MAW'S

Every Saturday night, stormy or clear, spring, summer, fall, or winter... Mee-Maw's Cajun Kitchen was the place to be.

Come suppertime, folks didn't hesitate. They jumped in beat-up pickup trucks, four-wheel-drive Jeeps, and two-seat John Deere Gators—as well as johnboats and pirogues—and traveling from Nebo, Jena, and Deville, and as far away as Dry Prong and Harrisonburg, descended on the little dockside restaurant on the western bank of Catahoula Lake. The only cuisine on their minds was down-home Creole and Cajun fare, and the only one—other than their very own mamas and grannies—who could cook it up and serve it right was Mee-Maw **Doucet.**

Mee-Maw was a fine, upstanding woman of sixty-three, held in high regard by all who knew her. She was kind and generous to all around her, a life-long member of the Catholic faith, and a benefactress to the poor and destitute in the area. Mee-Maw was a big woman, more bone and gristle than fat, standing six foot two in her stocking feet. Despite her age, her hair still held the jet blackness of her youth, with nary a strand of gray to be found, and her eyes were sharp and full of love and life.

And, hoo Lawd, could she ever cook! Shrimp and sausage gumbo, boiled crawfish, jambalaya, red beans and rice, maque choux, frog legs, gator tail, Creole chicken and okra, shrimp rémoulade, collard greens and fatback, deep-fried catfish, seafood étouffée, ham and goat cheese muffuletta, chicken cassoulet, pan-fried pork chops, red snapper with dirty rice, salt and sugar grits, yellow squash, and all manner of corn-bread—baked, fried, or rolled into golden hushpuppies. And there were desserts galore as well. Pecan pie, bread pudding with bourbon sauce, powdered beignets, glazed caramel pralines, Cajun king cake, black-berry cobbler, pumpkin tarte à la bouillie, Bananas Foster, and sweet potato pie.

Unbeknownst to many, though, was the fact that Mee-Maw Doucet had her fair share of trials and tribulations. She was married to a shiftless, no-account husband by the name of Leon Doucet—a tall, lanky fellow with a billy-goat beard and a golden ring in the lobe of his right ear. Leon was a man known to dabble in dubious business ventures such as trading in stolen goods and dealing in still-brewed corn liquor. He was surly and unkind to those who crossed his path and raised his ire, including his sweet and long-suffering wife. Mee-Maw also had a daughter named Babette who was tragically addicted to meth and heroin, and found herself in and out of the Louisiana correction facilities on a regular basis, as well as countless sessions of rehab that seemed to do no apparent good. Because of Bab's vices and incarcerations, it was left to Mee-Maw to raise her two grandchildren, Remy Lee and Aggie Mae. The two young'uns were Mee-Maw's pride and joy, and she would stop at nothing to provide for the two and protect them from following in the wayward footsteps of their misguided mother.

For many years, Mee-Maw endured her husband's abuse and blatant misbehavior, as many traditional Southern wives were taught from birth to do. It was when Remy and Aggie came to live in the Doucet house on the banks of Catahoula, however, that things took a bad turn... in worse ways than Mee-Maw could truly imagine.

Mee-Maw was hanging out the wash one afternoon, when little Remy ran across the back yard from behind the tool shed, his face red and bathed with tears.

The boy's eyes were full of pain and fear, and he limped as he ran past.

"What wrong with you, child?" Mee-Maw called out to him, fearing the worst. "Snake didn't bite you, did it?"

It was when he reached the porch steps that she saw the broad red welts on the back of his legs below the hem of his shorts. They were pink and inflamed, and whatever had caused them had drawn beads of blood in places.

"You get on in dat house and to your room!" a voice boomed from the far side of the yard. "And no supper for your belly tonight, you hear?"

Mee-Maw whirled to see her husband walking from the direction of the shed. The sleeves of his shirt were rolled to the elbows and he held the belt of his britches in one hand. It was the right—the one with PLEASURE tattooed across the knuckles. The left hand bore the word PAIN.

"What you do to the boy, Leon?" she snapped, her eyes flashing. "What cause you got to hurt his little legs that way?"

Leon Doucet squared his narrow shoulders and a half-grin curled up one side of his unshaven face like a yellow nightcrawler. "Caught him down yonder in the hollow… snooping around, being where he know he oughtn't. So I laid the leather to him. Taught him to stay clear of there… to keep his damn curiousness to himself!"

"You got no right…" Mee-Maw protested.

The man laughed. It was an ugly sound that came more from his black soul than his throat. "I got *every* right, woman! If that sorry-ass daughter of ours dumped them young'uns on our doorstep, to be fed and clothed, then they belong to me, the way I'd own a cat or dog. I'm their Pee-Paw, am I not? You coddle and spoil them every moment of every day, so it's up to me to raise them right. And, if it means, beating the living daylights outta 'em, then so be it!"

"They babies, Leon! It's a pure sin to treat them in such a way!"

"I'll treat the two any damn way I please!" the man told her. "Lay the strop to 'em and whale some discipline and respect into them like my paw did, and my pee-paw before him. And, if you come upholding for them and stand in my way, I'll give you a taste as well." He took the length of leather between both fists and made it pop loudly, like the crack of a bullwhip. Leon smiled cruelly. "You've had it before, in your younger years. You recall how I can make it sting and bruise. So, you'd best keep your grandmotherly concerns to yourself, chienne!"

The words hurt, but Mee-Maw stood tall and defiant, and swallowed them like a bitter pill she'd been given time and time again. Leon grinned, popped the belt again for emphasis, then turned and headed back to the hollow where he did his "business ventures" as he called them. Devil's work, pure and simple, it is, she thought to herself.

The woman felt the cheeks of her face flush red and hot with anger as she pinned up the last piece of clothing from the laundry basket. Then she went in to doctor the burning stripes on the back of poor Remy's legs with salve and a gentle, loving hand.

A week passed, then two. Mee-Maw knew that her household was under a hateful shadow and the ones who huddled and cowered in its oppressive shade were her two precious grandchildren.

A day didn't go by when they didn't show up at the dinner table with a scratch or bruise upon their arms or legs. When their grandfather sat down to eat, neither child lifted their eyes to acknowledge him. Their frightened gaze centered on the food upon their plates, which mostly sat there, growing cold, uneaten. Mee-Maw noticed that their weight began to fall off, ounce by ounce, and dark circles deepened around their eyes. It was plain to see that sleep eluded them at night, out of fret and worry...or pure and simple fear.

While shopping at the grocery store in town, Mee-Maw had run into their teacher, Mrs. Finch. In soft, but stern tones, she was told that Remy's and Aggie's grades had plunged to the point of failure, and that the girl trembled and bit back tears whenever she was called to do a problem on the blackboard and got it wrong. Mrs. Finch had also noticed the bruises and welts and was concerned for the children's safety. The way she said it, Mee-Maw knew she was being considerably restrained and feared that it wouldn't be long before the teacher called the sheriff and reported the abuse, which would open a nasty can of worms. Child Protective Services would come and take her two babies away, out of harm's way.

Mee-Maw considered doing something drastic. Maybe packing some clothes and toys up and leaving her home and husband. But she knew the kind of man Leon Doucet was... how vindictive and cruel he could be if he felt slighted or wronged. She wouldn't get past the county line before they were run off the road and at his mercy... of which there was none to speak of.

Then one Saturday morning, things happened that made her mind up for her and set the godly woman on a path she would have never considered taking in all her born days.

She was washing a sudsy sink full of dirty dishes, wanting to get some chores done before leaving for the restaurant at two o'clock to begin cooking for that night's crowd. She felt a tug on the strings of her apron and turned to find Remy standing there. His face was pale and scared, as if he'd seen something that had disturbed him, but he didn't rightly understand.

"What is it, baby?" she asked over her shoulder.

"Mee-Maw," he said. Remy's voice was low. A whisper. "You gotta come, Mee-Maw."

"You go on and play," she said with a smile, puzzling over his demeanor. "You know I gotta get this done, then take y'all to the babysitter so's I can go do tonight's cooking."

He tugged on the apron strings again, this time more urgently. His tiny hands clung to the cloth like a drowning man clutching a life preserver in stormy seas. "I fear for Aggie, Mee-Maw. She... she be hurting."

Mee-Maw's big, kind heart did a jittery dance in her chest. She pulled her hands from the suds and dried them with a dish towel. "Hurting, you say? What be the matter with her?"

"She asking for you to come. To the bathroom."

A dread unlike any the woman had ever know crept from her thundering heart, sickening her stomach, and making her bowels feel heavy and cold. She untied her apron and shucked it from her broad hips. "Remy, go in the living room, honey, and watch one of your cartoons."

"Mee-Maw!" moaned the boy, his eyes welling with tears.

She crouched and gave the child a hug. "It gonna be okay, mon bébé. I take good care of her, I promise that."

As the boy walked toward the living room, Mee-Maw turned and regarded the hallway that led to the door at the end. As she passed her sewing room and each bedroom, her legs felt heavy like concrete. She knew it must be the way condemned men felt as they walked their last steps to electric doom.

She reached the door and paused, then tapped softly on the panel.

"Aggie Mae... sweet girl," she said in a low voice. "Are you alright?"

"No," was all the child said.

"Are you hurt? What be the matter?"

Silence at first. Then a sob.

Mee-Maw's right hand hung at her side for a long, awful moment, not wanting to move. When it did, she turned the brass knob and went inside.

"Mee-Maw... shut the door behind you, please. I don't want to scare Remy no more."

It was then that the woman saw the little girl atop the commode, her reddened eyes staring at the floor. But, no... it was directed at her feet dangling above the floor... and the small panties pooled around her ankles.

Mee-Maw saw the awful shame and terror on Aggie's sweet face... saw the blood on white cotton... and she realized that a great evil had befallen her household.

Or, perhaps, even one that had been present for untold years, hidden discreetly and beyond her knowledge.

It was three o'clock that afternoon, when Leon burst through the back door of the Cajun Kitchen, mighty pissed off and angry.

He slammed the door behind him, his fists balled into hard knots of bone and gristle. "I was told that you needed me to come here and come quick," he grated between tobacco-stained teeth. "That you *demanded* that I drop what I was doing and be a-running!"

Mee-Maw stood at a thick chopping block in the center of the big kitchen floor and divided a long length of smoked sausage into quarters with a heavy meat cleaver. Her eyes were centered on her work. The late afternoon sun shone through the western window, glaring on the lenses of her black-rimmed glasses, obscuring the expression of her eyes.

"That I did," was all she said. Her voice was soft and gentle, but her hands were not. They brought the edge of the cleaver down with a heavy whack, separating the meat and biting into the hard hickory beyond.

Leon stomped up to the chopping block. He placed both hands on the edge and, although Mee-Maw was a big woman, towered over her threateningly. "You know very well not to be calling me from my work. Not on a Saturday, the busiest day of my week!" he told her. His words squeezed through the gaps of tightly-clenched teeth, hissing like an adder, filling her ears with venom. "You got nerve to be doing so, bitch... nerve that needs to be tamed and dealt with. I'll not lay a hand on you here, but when you get your ass home tonight..."

"You'll do what?" asked Mee-Maw softly. "What is it you'll be doing to me, Leon?"

It was at that moment that his wife turned her face to him and he saw her eyes behind the thick lenses her spectacles. He had seen eyes like that before—cold, flat, dark—peering at him from the murky waters of the bayou or amid the cattails and reeds at the edge of the lake. Reptile eyes. Like the hungry gator or the stepped-upon snake.

And, suddenly, he knew that she *knew.*

"Now, Mee-Maw..."

He was about to step back from her when she raised the cleaver once again. But this time it failed to cut pork. Instead, it sliced downward at an angle... well-placed and forceful... upon the column of his right wrist.

Leon Doucet stumbled away with a low moan building in his throat. He looked down at the stump of his wrist, at the brilliant spurting of blood, the pink tissue, the pale whiteness of exposed bone. Then he looked to the chopping block. The PLEASURE hand wiggled and flexed like a snapping turtle on its back, struggling to right itself. The calloused fingers worked, as if reaching, searching, for the appendage it had belonged to. But it strained and jittered in vain. Blind. Unaware of where its owner was and ignorant of the fact that it would never touch youthful flesh, in anger or lust, ever again.

"MEE-MAW!" wailed the lanky man as he sank to his knees, eyes pleading, face as pale as cooking lard. "What do you do? You've cut off my hand!"

The woman's face, once brimming with kindness and compassion, was now a mask of contempt and white-metal hatred. "I retribute upon you, Leon Doucet, you wicked man! I bring the Almighty's wrath upon you in full measure! Devil! Bringer of pain and perversion!"

As Leon's head swam, the veins of his wrist cast great, long spurts of blood across the hardwood floor, the chopping block, the front of Mee-Maw's clean, white apron. "I… I don't know what you be saying! What you're accusing me of!"

Mee-Maw glared at him. She tightened her fingers around the haft of the cleaver, then reached over and pulled a long-bladed butcher knife from a rack near the big, stainless-steel stove. "Liar! I always wondered why our sweet daughter Babette took the pathway she did… why she turned to drink and drugs, surrendered her body to the passions of men, tried to end her life time after time. Now I know. Now I understand the agony and shame within her blackened soul. And, if my eyes had not been opened, sweet, little Aggie would have become just like her. And perhaps even poor Remy, if you'd turned your foul affections toward him as well!"

The flash of the cleaver came once again, whistling downward forcefully, aiming for the center of Leon's face. He brought his left hand up, to block the blow. The honed edge sliced cleanly through flesh and bone, hacking away four of his fingers. The stubs of the bleeding knuckles read—and screamed—PAIN.

Leon began to skuttle backward across the floor. How far away was the back door? Ten feet? Eight? He was afraid to turn his head to check. Mee-Maw was advancing slowly… huge, a mountain of righteous retribution with hands full of honed steel.

"The Bible, it says, if a part of your body offends you, you should cut it off," the woman told him. "And, I'll be telling you, there's so much of you that offends me, I can scarcely count." A grin crossed Mee-Maw's flushed face. The kind and benevolent eyes that normally shone behind the lenses of her glasses had grown dark and dangerous. "Oh, but I will count them… bit by bit, and piece by piece!"

Around four-thirty that afternoon, the employees of the Cajun Kitchen began to arrive, to prepare for that night's crowd. As everyone knew and anticipated, Mee-Maw's doors opened promptly at six o'clock, not a second earlier or later.

The first ones to arrive were the Kitchen's number one chef, Big Pete Mangrum, and two waitresses, Corinne Blanchard and Julianne Guidry, who was sixteen and new to the staff. Big Pete unlocked the front door, then locked it back behind them when they came in. As they walked through the big dining room with its three dozen tables, an odor hit their nostrils. Thick and cloying, and more than unpleasant.

"Whoo-boy!" said Corinne. "What is that I be smelling?"

"Not particularly sure," murmured Big Pete. But he had butchered enough hogs in his daddy's barn since the age of twelve to recognize the coppery stench for what it was.

They reached the double doors that led to the restaurant's kitchen. "You ladies stay out here for a moment."

Startled, Julianne nodded, her dark ponytail bobbing. Corinne, who was thirty-two and rougher than a cob, frowned at the big man and cocked an eyebrow. "Naw, I think I'll be going in with you."

Big Pete didn't have time to argue the point. He had been mowing his yard earlier that afternoon when he'd seen Leon Doucet speeding down the highway in his primer gray Chevy pickup, looking red-faced and madder than hell. Pete traded worried glances with Corinne, then both took a deep breath and went through the swinging doors together.

They were relieved to see Mee-Maw at a preparation counter at the far side of the kitchen with her back to them. She had a long-bladed knife, chopping something up and tossing it into the big gumbo kettle on one of the eyes of the cookstove.

"Mee-Maw!" he said with sigh. "Thank God you be okay!"

The big man took a step inside and the sole of his shoe slid in something wet and slick. He looked down and was shocked to see that the kitchen floor was covered in fresh blood.

He looked over at Corinne. The waitress was as pale as a fish belly, looking as though she wished she'd heeded Big Pete's request to remain in the dining hall.

The chef took a couple steps backward, opened the twin doors a crack, and whispered to the teenager in a low voice. "Julianne... get on that phone of yours and call the sheriff's office. Tell 'em to git out here quick."

When he was satisfied that the girl was doing as he asked, he started carefully across the floor toward his boss. He looked down at the puddles on the linoleum floor and spotted something lying there.

It was a man's ear with a shiny, gold ring hooked through the lobe.

"Mee-Maw," he said calmly. "Where is Leon?"

The old woman turned and looked at him over her broad shoulder. Her face was sweaty and as pale as biscuit dough. Through the blood-specked lenses of her glasses, her eyes held a wild light, glassy and hot, like someone in the throes of a high fever. "Leon?" she said, thinking for a moment. "Oh... I believe he be outside on the patio."

Big Pete looked at the waitress, as if saying "Stay here". Corinne looked back with "I ain't going nowhere" in her eyes.

Mee-Maw paid him no mind as he passed her and opened the back door. Big Pete stepped onto the flagstone patio and looked around. The fenced-in space was completely empty... except for the big iron boiling pot where crawfish and crabs were prepared for the big, Saturday night feast. Mee-Maw already had it going. A fire had been lit underneath and the water within was bubbling and boiling at high heat, causing the big iron lid on top to jitter and rattle as steam vented past the edges.

The smell that hit him then was downright hellacious. "Sweet Lady of the Assumption!" he declared. Then, grabbing a pair of heavy leather gloves from a metal rack near the door, he ran over and lifted the heavy lid from the cauldron.

Within the boiling water danced the red-pink bodies of crawfish and the oval shells of blue crab. But there were other things churning in the water as well. Things that never should have been there.

A long, blistered foot with curled, yellow toenails.

A handless arm, tattooed and lanky, cleaved off at the shoulder.

A heart, a kidney, a long length of innards, twisting and turning like a puffy gray snake.

As Big Pete watched, something large and round bobbed to the surface and stared him flat in the face. It was the scalded head of Leon Doucet, the flesh cooked and peeling, the eyes blood-red and swollen to the point of popping. The whiskered mouth yawned wide in a silenced scream. The organ that would have vented his terror was no longer within the gaping maw. It appeared a few seconds later, flipping and turning round and round, torn free by the root and licking at its master's roasted ear.

The Cajun chef lifted his eyes from the awful contents of the boiling pot and, looking through the back window, got a good look at the thing Mee-Maw whittled down and tossed into the gumbo. And it wasn't smoked andouille, that was for damn sure.

Big Pete Mangrum returned the lid to the big iron pot and heard the wail of a siren in the distance. He knew in his heart that Mee-Maw's place had seen its last Saturday night and that he—and everyone else on the staff—would be in search of a new job bright and early Monday morning.

And Mee-Maw? Knowing the sheriff and his notorious hankering for Cajun vittles, she'd likely be wearing a DayGlo orange apron, cooking up a storm at the county jail.

CAT DADDY FEVER

1974 was the summer I had Cat Daddy Fever.

I was thirteen that year. Becky McGhee. Strawberry-blonde, skinny as a swamp crane, hopelessly homely, or so I thought so. Not pretty like a lot of the other girls in my eighth-grade class. Folks in Bogalusa Parish called me a true-to-the-bone tomboy and there was no denying that I was. I could run a trotline for mudcats and solo-paddle a canoe across the bayou when I was eight… rebuild a carburetor and drive the stick of my daddy's old Willys jeep by the age of twelve. Didn't make me all that popular with the boys… especially with them knowing how Papa was and that he'd just soon part their hair with a shotgun than let them set a toenail in our yard to come visiting.

Mama died in '71. She was working at the shirt factory over in Covington and dropped dead at her sewing machine, stitching bra straps. A vein had opened up in her head and she was gone before she hit the concrete floor. It was terribly hard on me and twice as hard on Papa. He was already a hard-drinking man with a troublesome disposition, and Mama's passing tripled that ugliness in him. It didn't help none that I was the spitting image of my mother and every time he looked at me, he saw her walking around, like a ghost that refused to go to glory.

Papa was a truck driver by trade, so he found his escape on the road. He pretty much left me home to fend for myself nine months out of the twelve, mailed me money every other week for food and paying the bills. Everyone in Bogalusa Parish knew I was out there on the edge of Black Bayou all by myself, but nobody made a big deal of it, not even the law. Most were scared to. They were afraid my father would come home and find me in foster care somewhere and there would be hell to pay, so they let it be.

But you don't want to hear about me and my lousy childhood, do you? You want to know about who—or what—Cat Daddy was… and why I was so obsessed with finding him that summer.

There was a big monster craze back in the early '70s. For me, a lot of it was sparked by those old black-and-white monster movies that were shown on the Saturday night Creature Feature on Channel 4 out of Baton Rouge. Movies like The Amazing Colossal Man, Frankenstein Meets the Wolfman, The Mole People, The Incredible Shrinking Man and dozens more. My favorite was Creature from the Black Lagoon. I was flat-out struck on the Gillman that summer. I cut pictures of him from Famous Monsters of Filmland magazine and hung them on my bedroom wall, even bought the Aurora monster model kit at the dime store in town and glued and painted it. I used the glow-in-the-dark pieces that came with it, just so I could wake up in the middle of the night and see him there on my nightstand in the dark, watching over me.

And there were all those books I checked out of the school library and bought off the paperback rack at LaFleur's Drugstore. Alfred Hitchcock story collections, Ripley's Believe or Not!, and a book called *Carrie* by a new writer named King. And there were plenty of books about true sightings of UFOs, Bigfoot, and the Loch Ness Monster. Of course, in my mind, all that was real and irrefutable. After all, in between all the eerie and horrifying encounters, there were grainy black-and-white photos to prove they existed. I didn't let on at school that I was crazy about monsters and cryptids and such, though. That was supposed to be a boy thing, not something girls my age should be dwelling on. I never took them to school, for fear that I'd be sent to the guidance counselor for a discussion about "lady-like qualities".

Black Bayou had its own monster, one that was talked about quietly around midnight campfires, by the old men who played checkers out front of the courthouse, and by the kids on the playground at school. It was an East Louisiana version of the Boogeyman, one that had been a source of tall tales and swamp folklore for well over a century, maybe more. The mysterious and notorious Cat Daddy.

I recalled my Granny McGhee telling me about him when I was scarcely six-years old, and her words stuck with me like a leech that had latched on and wouldn't let go. *"Ol' Cat Daddy, he's been stalking the bayou for longer than anyone can rightly remember,"* she had said. *"My own grandpappy told me tales of the creature and the horrors he brought to the Parish back in the olden days. Told me a story of how a great beast—a monstrous gar—rose up out of the depths of Horseshoe Bay at the edge of town shortly after the War Between the States, conjured by a dark-haired demon man. Before it could destroy the Parish, Ol' Cat Daddy jumped upon its back, reached around its hideous head, and clawed its eyes blind! It was said that a black mojo man called a cloud of locusts down from the heavens and stripped the gar's bones clean of flesh, but Cat Daddy escaped… diving deep into the water before he could suffer a similar fate!"*

Granny's description of Cat Daddy pretty much matched the one I'd heard all my life. *"Ol' Daddy, he be half-man and half-blackwater catfish. Tall and thin, well over seven feet in height… covered in black scales and sharp fins upon his arms and legs, his underbelly pale and slick as a baby's ass-end. His head is that of a mudcat, grotesquely huge and broad from side to side. The eyes are pale gray and fearful to look upon, the mouth wide enough to swallow a human head whole, and long, fleshy whiskers dangle down from his chin and cheeks. They say Cat Daddy possesses the strength of ten stout men and that his hands are webbed betwixt the fingers and its claws sharp enough to cleave meat from the bone with no effort a'tall!"*

That story, and others that I'd heard over the years, only piqued my interest in the swamp legend. By the time July of '74 rolled around, my need to hunt down and lay eyes upon Cat Daddy had reached a fever pitch. There was no one there to stop me or talk me out of it; Papa was making cross-country runs from Slidell to California that summer and wouldn't likely be back in the parish until early September. I simply had to prove to myself that Black Bayou's version of the Gill-man was a living, breathing reality and not something made up and embellished over decades of storytelling.

But I wasn't stupid enough to go out looking for him in the marshlands alone.

I had to find someone to go with me. Someone who was just as serious as I was about locating Cat Daddy's lair. Someone I could trust, with my very life, if it came down to that.

As it turned out, I found two.

The first was Jaybo Sutton. He was tall, pert near as skinny as I was, and had the prettiest dark brown eyes of any boy I'd ever known. He was also from Jamaica and his skin was black as coal on a moonless night. Jaybo was on the basketball team at school, but not one of the popular kids. He seemed much happier hanging around the lunchroom table with the bookworms and science nerds... and me. He, too, had a thing about monsters and weird stuff. He was an "aficionado of the macabre," and always said with pride.

I had a humongous crush on him that summer. Just looking at that bright smile shining from that beautiful dark face of his made a shiver run down my spine, past my tailbone, and end up, well, you know where. Some nights I'd lay in bed and imagine that we'd get married someday and have a passel of babies. I wouldn't have dared admit that to my father, though. He was a nasty bigot—more so than Archie Bunker on TV—and had a deep distrust and hatred of folks of color that I could never rightly understand. If he'd known I had the hots for a black boy, he would have tanned my hide something awful... so I kept it to myself.

My second-best friend in eighth grade was Dusty Ashburn. Dusty was overweight by thirty or forty pounds, had hair the color of tobacco spit, and wore thick-lensed, horn-rimmed glasses that magnified his eyes like Burgess Meredith on that atomic bomb episode of *The Twilight Zone*. He was super smart and painfully quiet and shy... except for when he was around me and Jaybo. Then his personality seemed to burst forth like a butterfly from a cocoon. He was a sensitive kid and his voice and the manner in which he talked reminded me more of me than Jaybo. I found out later, midway through high school, that he was gay. I was the only one he told. It was 1976 and no one had the nerve to come "out" like they do now... not in rural Louisiana anyway. I could see the naked fear in his eyes when he spilled the beans and the surprise and relief when I put my arms around him and hugged him tightly. He cried on my shoulder, as though a burden had been lifted off him, which made me love him even more than before. As you may guess, I didn't tell Papa about Dusty and his "secret", either. He was always spouting hatred about "queers" and "niggers", especially when liquored up. It hurt my heart something awful and I'd cry in my bedroom and hate him for the way he was. So, it was best that I said as little about my friends—and what they were—as possible.

It was on a Saturday night in late June, while we watched *Revenge of the Creature* on the black-and-white Zenith in my living room, that I told them what I had in mind.

"I want to go out into the swamp," I said aloud, during an

Alka-Seltzer commercial. "Hoped y'all would go with me. Take my canoe and go find him."

"Find who?" asked Dusty, chasing a mouthful of Cheetos with a swallow of Dr Pepper.

I hesitated, my heart pounding in my chest. "Cat Daddy."

Jaybo had been drinking 7 Up and it sprayed out his nostrils like a fire hose when he heard what I said. *"What?* You can't be serious!"

"Serious as a heart attack," I told him. "Gonna see for myself if he's real or not. Maybe take that old eight-millimeter camera of Papa's and get him on film. And good footage, too… not some out-of-focus piece of bullshit like that one of Bigfoot strolling through the woods in California."

"Even if you went looking for Cat Daddy, you'd never find him," Dusty proclaimed. "Every Cajun swamper in these has tried to track him down with no luck. And that's been for a hundred years or more. Why do you think you'll do any better?"

"Because my Granny McGhee told me where to look," I told them both. "Said he hung out near Bergeron's sandbar."

Jaybo's Adam's apple bobbed in his throat like a Duncan yoyo. "That's way back yonder in Black Bayou! We'd be plumb crazy to go out in the boonies in that old canoe of yours. The place is crawling with gator and cottonmouth!"

"Well," I said in mock disgust, "if you're too pussy to take the chance…"

"You bet I'm pussy!" said Dustin. "So pussy I'd stink like Mee-Maw's fish fry on a Saturday night. I ain't going in there looking for that fish-monster, no ma'am! You know how many men have gone looking for him and never came back alive? Thirty-eight and counting, or so the fellers down at the bait shop claim."

"Besides," said Jaybo, "no critter can live as long as folks have been talking about Cat Daddy. I've even heard that Andrew Jackson and his troops happened across him on their march to N'awlins, and that was way back in 1814. If there was such a thing, it up and died a long time ago."

"Well, you ain't gonna talk me out of it," I told them. "I'll just go by myself and leave your sorry, scaredy-cat asses behind. I'm going out into the Bayou and track him down, then take a picture of him that'll get me on the evening news and maybe even the Johnny Carson Show!"

Jaybo and Dusty looked at one another, downright exasperated by the commotion I was causing. "Even if we did decide to go," Dusty finally said, "what kinda story are we making up? Bergeron's Bar is twelve miles down the channel. We'd end up having to camp for the night and come back the next day. And I know my mama ain't gonna let me go out there to catch some godawful disease or get my leg bitten off by Pa Gator!"

"Just tell your folks that we're having a sleepover in my back yard," I said. "That we're going to roast Oscar Mayers and marshmallows over the fire and tell ghost stories until none of us can sleep a wink."

Jaybo looked doubtful. "I don't know. My mom is getting kind of suspicious lately... says we shouldn't be doing sleepovers anymore, what with you being a growing girl and all. Says it ain't appropriate."

"Aw!" I said, rolling my eyes. "We been doing it since we were nine!"

"Yeah, but you didn't have titties and a burning bush south of your belly button to worry about back then," Dusty declared, laughing. "Jaybo's mama don't want no grandbabies to take care of before y'all graduate junior high."

My ears got redder than a cayenne pepper when he said that. Jimbo grabbed a harvest-gold pillow off the couch and held it menacingly in front of Dusty's moon pie face. "Why don't I just smother you right now and your mama won't have to worry about chucking around no grandbabies at all!"

Dusty was heavyset but fast enough to dodge Jaybo's attack. "Ain't planning on having nary a one anyway!" he said. It wasn't until we had our talk years later that I fully understood what he meant by that.

"Y'all just ask, okay?" I urged. "Don't make out that it's some big deal. Just say we want one more campout before the summer's over and done with. Nobody's likely to drive out here and check on us anyway."

My two pals stared at me hopelessly, then agreed to my scheme.

"If we go out there and get ourselves killed, I'm never gonna forgive you," said Jaybo. Then he smiled and winked at me. And my heart melted like butter.

With that settled, we went back to watching our Creature movie and eating our snacks. I really wanted to scoot down the couch cushions and sit next to Jaybo, and something told me he wanted to do the same. But we didn't. It would've been weird doing it in front of Dusty... who would have made it his mission in life to never let us live it down.

We decided to take our journey into Black Bayou on the Friday and Saturday after Fourth of July weekend. Both Jaybo's and Dusty's mothers insisted they be back to their houses at suppertime on Saturday evening, so they'd be ready for church bright and early Sunday morning. I hadn't been to church since Mama died, so I didn't have that to worry about. I suppose I really had no excuse, since the church bus passed by the house, but it didn't seem right going without Mama. And, besides, I'd outgrown all my pretty clothes and found no reason to buy new ones in the past three years.

When the weekend finally came around, we were all excited about it, despite Jaybo's and Dusty's earlier reservations. We packed a couple of backpacks with food and snacks: hot dog wieners and buns; marshmallows, graham crackers, and Hershey bars for making s'mores; Pringles; Little Debbie cakes; and plenty of Slim Jims. There was a Styrofoam cooler, too, stocked with ice-cold Dr Pepper, Coca Cola, 7 Up, and A&W Root Beer. I took my daddy's transistor radio—the big one with the four D-batteries and the telescoping antenna—and, although the boys didn't know it, I'd taken my father's .45 pistol… the one he'd smuggled home from Vietnam in his duffle bag between dog-eared issues of *Playboy*. I didn't think we'd end up needing it, but it was foolish going out into the swamp without something to defend yourself with.

It was a wonder that Jaybo's and Dusty's parents even allowed to them out of the house that weekend, because there had been some bad things going on in the parish lately. Folks' houses being broken into and things stolen from their yards and sheds. And someone had broken into Mr. LaFleur's drugstore late one night, not knowing that the owner was still there. They'd cracked the pharmacist across the back of the skull with a monkey wrench and gave him a severe concussion that laid him up in the hospital for the better part of a week. They'd gotten away with a variety of prescription drugs, five hundred and eighty-nine dollars out of the cash register, and a jumbo Trojan Pleasure Pack of assorted condoms. Some folks in the parish said it was the Trahan Brothers, Dale and Donnie, and their buddy, Earl LeBouef. The Trahans were no-account white trash (at least that was Papa's assessment) and were known to brew homemade shine and grow marijuana in unknown places out in the bayou. LeBouef had spent twelve years in the state penitentiary in Angola for kidnapping a child from a county fair and raping her. He'd gotten out on parole for good behavior, but folks who knew him bet that Earl would get the urge and try it again before the year was over.

We pitched a tent in my back yard and built a fake campfire out of stones and sticks. It was strictly for looks, in case someone did come around to check on us. Then we loaded our gear in my fifteen-foot canoe and headed into the swamp. When we started out, Jaybo was oaring at the bow, me at the stern, and Dusty sat squarely in the middle of the boat, guarding the food and drinks. As we navigated the winding channel of Black Bayou, we turned on the radio and sang along to Three Dog Night, Led Zeppelin, and Lynyrd Skynyrd. A time or two, an ABBA song came on and I wanted to sing the lyrics, but I didn't, knowing the guys would tease the hell out of me.

As the morning drew on into afternoon, the sun overhead became obscured by the overlapping branches of cypress and weeping willow. The heavy mats of stringy, gray Spanish moss that clung to the limbs blocked out the sunlight even more and we found ourselves in dappled shade most of the time. Every now and then we'd see gators sleeping on the banks, waiting for nightfall, or water moccasins swimming across the murky water. Once, a snake stuck its head up and peeked curiously over the bow, but Jaybo chased it away with the paddle of his oar.

As evening drew near, I figured that we'd gone nine of the twelve miles between my house and Bergeron's Bar. The radio began to cut out and emit static so badly that we turned it off to save the batteries. We talked about new horror movies that would be showing at Big Vern's Drive-In Theatre on Highway 1--flicks like *Lucifer's Women, It's Alive!, The Texas Chain Saw Massacre,* and *Madhouse* with Vincent Price.

We also talked about starting high school in September. We talked it up big and acted like we were ready, but we all knew we weren't. We'd heard bad stuff about upperclassmen harassing and hazing freshmen, especially those that didn't fit into their particular social class. Dusty didn't say it, but I think he was scared shitless to make the transition. He had been bullied enough in grade school. It was bound to be twice as bad once he hit the crowded halls of Bogalusa High.

It was nearly dark when we reached the long, narrow island of Bergeron's Bar in the furthest reaches of Black Bayou.

We were glad to get there, because the last hour on the water was the most troubling. As the sun set and gold and crimson light filtered through the thick moss and leaves overhead, it nearly grew too gloomy to see where we were going. Jaybo had brought a Coleman lantern, but it was only half full of kerosene, so we thought it best to not light it until absolutely necessary. A feeling of uneasiness and dread descended upon the three of us and we didn't talk much, just listened to the sounds around us and studied the dense shadows that surrounded the backwater channel. None of us said it aloud, but we felt like someone, or *something*, was watching us. Not critters like gators, snakes, coons, or possums… but something more aware, more clever. Maybe a man… maybe not.

Once, before it got too dark, we pulled up to the bank and I got out to pee. My bladder was full and I felt like I was about to bust… otherwise, we'd kept going. I stepped onto the mossy bank and squatted in a clump of ferns, while Jaybo and Dusty looked the other way. I had a hard time going and, since I was next to the base of a sour gum tree, I took my Case knife out of my shorts pocket and carved something in the bark, just to pass the time. B.M. LOVES J.S. I didn't carve it high up where Jaybo could actually see it, although I wouldn't have minded if he had.

Just before I pulled up my drawers and shorts, something cracked in the woods beyond the sour gum, like someone stepping on a dead branch in the thicket. I peered off into the shadows, but could see nothing. Still, I felt like I was being watched and it spooked me. I jumped back into the boat, told Jaybo to paddle like the Devil with Jesus on his heels, and we were away from there.

Okay, it sort of feels like I'm stalling here, doesn't it? Not getting to the point and telling you about our time on the sandbar and what happened there. Maybe, deep down inside, I don't want to think about it or relive it.

Maybe, in another way, I don't fully understand what really happened during that awful half hour and how we escaped Bergeron's Bar with our lives.

We stepped out of the canoe and all three of us tugged it onto the edge of the narrow island in the middle of the channel. Then we studied Bergeron's Bar and began to wonder why the hell we were there.

It was about forty feet in length and half that distance wide, made of sand and brown creek stone. The only thing that was there was a scattering of driftwood and the stump of an ancient cypress tree smack dab in the middle. I'd had it in my mind that there would be an outcropping of mossy stone there, maybe with a cave opening leading to Cat Daddy's underground lair. But there was nothing like that at all. Just the broad stump with thick roots running from its base in all directions.

Jaybo rubbed at the sore muscles of his arms. "You mean I rowed all day long for nothing?" he snapped.

"Yeah!" said Dusty. "So, where is this doggone fish creature of yours?"

As a chorus of peep frogs and crickets sang around us, I felt my heart sink and my temper flare at the same time. "Hell, I don't know! Maybe he'll show up sometime tonight." Just standing there with them glaring at me like that, I felt a wave of disappointment and guilt rush over me. I also felt like walking up and giving them both a kick in the nuts for making me feel like shit.

I think Jaybo could see how pissed I was, so he tried to defuse the situation. "Well, we're here until morning, so let's make the best of it. We'll build a fire, eat supper, and have fun. It'll be like camping in your back yard, only we're stuck in the middle of a spooky old swamp."

A loon screamed somewhere in the darkness. We all jumped and then burst out laughing. Together, we pulled the backpacks and the cooler from the canoe, then built a fire with the driftwood. Curiously, I went over and examined the stump. I was surprised to find that it was hollow. The innards were gone, but it was filled to the top with dead leaves and strands of withered Spanish moss.

I reached in to grab a handful to help kindle the fire and my fingertips hit something solid a few inches down. I swept the leaves and moss aside and was surprised to find that someone had wedged the plastic lid of a bucket inside the stump. It was as though they had done so to hide something underneath and protect it from the weather.

"Hey!" I told the boys. "Come take a look!"

Soon, they were next to me. We looked at one another, feeling that maybe our trip hadn't been a wasted one after all.

"What do you think is underneath?" asked Dusty.

"Who knows?" I said. "What are we waiting for?" Then I reached down, wrestled with the lid, and pulled it loose. Evening had darkened to dusk and all we could see at the bottom of the hollow stump was shadow. Jaybo took a book of matches from the pocket of his jeans, lifted the chimney of the Coleman lantern, and lit the wick. Then he held it over and illuminated what was inside.

We were shocked to find four quart-sized Mason jars sitting at the bottom. My heart pounded in suspense as I reached down and drew them out one by one. The first held a number of five-, ten-, and twenty-dollar bills, along with a handful of change in the bottom. The other three held bottles and vials of pills and capsules. Along with the jars was a brown paper bag. I opened it and saw an open box of rubbers, or that's what I thought them to be, because I'd heard tell of them but never actually seen one before.

"Shitfire!" said Dusty. "That's the loot from Mr. LaFleur's drugstore!"

The moment he said that, a cold feeling of dread shot through me and I heard something echo across the water to the north of the sandbar, and not very far away at all. I recognized the sound immediately. It was a metallic sound... the working of a rifle's lever action. My father had an old Winchester .44-40 and it sounded identical when you jacked a cartridge into the breech.

"Y'all stand stone still," warned a voice in the darkness. "Set that stuff back down in the stump. You run and I'll put a rifle slug clean through your backbone."

"He ain't lying," said another. "He'll do it and not think a thing about it."

We stood as still as statues and listened. We had been so excited about finding the treasure in the tree stump, that we'd failed to hear the sound of a boat skimming the still water of Black Bayou from the direction of town. Soon, the boat reached Bergeron's Bar and three men stepped onto the sand and silt. They took a few steps toward us until the dancing light of the campfire revealed them.

Two were brothers from the looks of them, sort of small in height and thin, with shaggy black hair and beards. The third was a big, broad-shouldered man in wading boots, jeans, and a dingy white t-shirt. His face was broad and clean-shaven, and his hair was the color of rust on a door hinge. An ugly scar ran diagonally down his face from above his right eyebrow, across the bridge of his nose, and came to an end at the left-hand corner of his mouth. He had a revolver stuck in his belt—a .38 Smith & Wesson from the looks of it—and a sheathed knife on his right hip—a skinning knife with a staghorn handle.

I'd never seen those three men before in my life, but I knew them from all the talk I'd heard in Bogalusa Parish. The two dark-haired brothers were Dale and Donnie Trahan, which meant the third man was undoubtedly the ex-con child rapist, Earl LeBouef.

We didn't move a muscle, unsure of what to do next. Here we'd discovered their cache of stolen money and drugs right when they'd come to retrieve it. My heart pounded wildly, for I knew it was a good bet that we wouldn't be leaving Bergeron's Bar alive.

"Donnie, you stand back there with the boat," LeBouef told the man with the Winchester rifle. "If you see 'em make a wrong move, shoot 'em."

The man nodded and remained where he was, while the other two

                        Ronald Kelly

approached us. The big man drew the revolver from his waistband and grinned. He was missing several teeth, while all the others were stained dingy and brownish-yellow from smoking.

"What the hell y'all doing out here?" he asked. His voice was rough and gravelly, as though pebbles and grit were stuck in his vocal cords, rubbing one against the other. "Came looking for our stash, did you? Well, you sure as shit found it… and us, too."

"What do you wanna do with 'em?" This from the other one, Dale Trahan, who held a double-barreled twelve-gauge in both hands.

"Can't let 'em go, that's for sure," said Earl. He stepped forward and kicked at our ankles until we dropped to our knees. "Put your hands on your heads. Not that you're much of a threat. A fat-ass, a nigger, and a skinny girl…but a pretty one at that."

The way he said that made my stomach squirm like a nest of nightcrawlers.

"Dale, you walk around to the far side of that stump," he instructed. When Dale had done as he was told, Earl chuckled to himself. "Okay, now this is what's gonna happen." He stepped up, grabbed a handful of Jaybo's afro, and wrenched his head upward so he could look him square in the eyes. He placed the muzzle of the .38 against Jaybo's forehead, a couple of inches above the bridge of his nose. "I'm gonna blow your brains out, peckerwood, then I'm gonna do the same to tubby boy here."

Jaybo and Dusty began to cry like babies. I began to cry, too, because I knew I'd screwed up, big time. Jaybo's words came back to haunt me. *If we go out there and get yourselves killed, I'm never gonna forgive you.*

"I-I'm sorry, Jaybo," I moaned.

He cut his eyes, full tears, my way. "Becky… I-I…"

Say it, I thought. *Please!*

But he never got the chance. Before he could, Earl LeBouef lifted the stubby barrel of the gun and clubbed him atop the head. Jaybo cried out and dropped to the rocky earth, crying even harder than before. I looked over at the backpack I'd brought, with Papa's gun inside. It seemed utterly useless, as though it were a million miles from my reach.

The big man looked over at me and cocked his head. "You like this little nigger boy, don't you? Well, you can watch while I put a hole in his head, and then do the same for the other one. You, however, well, we might just take you home with us, baby doll. Keep you for a while to cook and clean. Attend to our needs." His ugly grin broadened. "Yeah, we got all kinds of needs, don't we boys?"

The Trahan Brothers agreed and laughed along with him. I felt like

I was going to puke. I thought about begging him to kill me, too. But it was plain to see that they had other plans for me.

"I know your daddy, girl," Earl told me. "And I know for a fact that he'll be on the road for a while. We could keep you two or three years, and no one would be the wiser. They'll just think you up and ran off somewhere."

I realized he was right. They could keep me locked up as their slave forever and no one in the parish would give a damn.

"Alright now," said the ex-con, "time to get this done." He placed the muzzle of the revolver against the top of Jaybo's head and thumbed back the hammer.

I squeezed my eyes shut and sobbed, grieving over the death of my beloved before the shot was even fired.

As it turned out, it never was. At least not at Jaybo and Dusty.

Donnie Trahan cried out, startled. The two men standing over us turned in time to see their partner in crime being pulled backward into the darkness. The Winchester dropped from his hands and clattered on the stones of the sandbar. There was a splash and a gurgle, and he was gone.

"What the shit!" cussed Dale. "Where'd he go?"

Something strange happened then. The frogs and crickets around us grew quiet and made no sound. The night became as silent as it was dark.

Earl lifted the gun from Jaybo and aimed it toward the spot where the man had stood moments before. "Donnie! You okay?" he yelled out, but it was clear to see that he knew very well that Donnie was probably dead, snatched off his feet and drowned beneath the dark waters of Black Bayou.

For a long instant, we all were all frozen to the spot--me and the boys on our knees, and the two remaining men standing on opposite sides of the hollow stump.

Then, abruptly, Dale Trahan began to shriek at the top of his lungs.

We turned our heads and looked.

And, oh God, what we saw...

A dark form, lean and impossibly tall, its black scales glistening in the flickering glow of the campfire, had crept up and grabbed Dale from behind. The man thrashed and fought, but there was no breaking free. One of the creature's webbed hands closed over his screaming face, flexing, tightening, anchoring its long, black claws deeply into muscle and sinew. Then, with a sickening rending and tearing of fragile flesh, the clawed hand ripped Dale Trahan's bearded face clean off.

For a horrifying moment, his gore-bathed skull shrieked, long and shrill, the eyes still staring from their dark, lidless sockets in complete and utter terror. In response, the thing flung his flaccid face aside and ended his agony, more out of cruel pleasure than mercy. The monster closed its other hand around the column of Dale's throat and snapped his neck with a brittle crack, nearly twisting his head from his shoulders.

The Smith & Wesson boomed as Earl fired at the towering creature point blank. As the thing leapt over the cypress stump and faced the man, the gun emptied its cylinder, but the bullets seemed to have little effect on it. They seemed to hit its dark scales and flatten. One even ricocheted, returning in the direction from which it was fired. Earl screamed as it punctured his left eye, blinding him.

Kneeling there, unable to move, I stared up and saw the being I had come in search of. It was a dozen times more terrifying than the stories Granny McGhee had described. Its long, lean arms rippled with corded muscle, as though eels writhed and squirmed beneath the black scales. The massive fish head sat atop the monster's broad shoulders, its huge eyes bulging and slick with mucus. The broad mouth gasped for air, causing the long, fleshy whiskers to bob up and down, clear to the gray nipples of its pale chest.

When the gun had expelled its contents and grown useless, Earl staggered backward and threw it at the thing known as Cat Daddy. The creature caught the firearm in midair and crushed it between its long fingers as though it were made of aluminum foil.

Before he could turn and run, Cat Daddy was upon him. I watched, half in terror, half in morbid fascination, as the monster's hands grabbed the ex-con by the shoulders, the claws slicing deeply, penetrating muscle and bone. Then, with a hoarse bellow, the fish man opened its arms wide and ripped Earl LeBouef completely in half. The two sides of the man stood upright for a long moment, then dropped to the stones of the sandbar as Cat Daddy relinquished its hold.

I buried my head in my hands and cowered, waiting for my turn.

But it never came.

I sensed the massive bulk of the brute standing over me, smelled the dank and sour stench of his fishy flesh. Then one of its wickedly-clawed hands reached down and tenderly stroked my strawberry-blonde hair.

After that, I heard heavy footfalls, followed by the splash of its departure.

Lifting my face, I looked around. Our savior, the centuries-old legend of Black Bayou, was nowhere to be seen.

The rest of the night the three of us huddled before the fire, frightened but thankful to be alive. Unlike those who lay in ruined pieces around us.

The next morning, at the first light of dawn, we took the four Mason jars, launched the canoe, and made our way home.

Jaybo Sutton and I got married a few months after graduating high school.

During the wedding, Papa showed up stinking drunk and started a ruckus in the church foyer. Jaybo knocked him out cold and Jaybo's father and uncle carried him outside and dumped him into the back of his jeep. That was the last time I laid eyes on my father. He died of prostate cancer in 2012. I'd like to say I forgave him and attended the funeral, but I didn't. In my eyes, what made him my daddy had died a long time ago.

We moved to Shreveport, where Jaybo got a job managing a grocery store and I worked as a teller in a bank. We had our passel of babies—five in all—who grew up to be doctors and lawyers and soldiers. They and the grandbabies threw us a big party a couple of months ago to celebrate mine and Jaybo's forty-fifth wedding anniversary.

After attending college, Dusty Ashburn moved to Seattle, saying he wanted to "be as far away from Louisiana as possible, to be with folks of his own kind". We receive Christmas cards from him every now and then, and follow him on social media. The last we heard he was touring Europe with his husband, Jonathan. They seem happy and content. Just knowing that makes me happy in return.

Toward the end of May of this year, we drove back to Bogalusa Parish to put flowers on Mama's grave.

The town cemetery is at the edge of town, a stone's throw from the dark waters of Black Bayou. The field is bright and grassy, with rows of mausoleums and above-ground lawn crypts. The earth is so marshy in that area that below-ground burial is discouraged. More times than can be remembered, heavy rains had flooded the bayou and caskets and vaults had risen to the surface.

We got there in late afternoon. The sun was still over the crest of the trees, but long shadows were beginning to stretch across the granite walls and lids of the burial sites. I walked to Mama's grave, while Jaybo opened the car trunk and retrieved the yellow Dollar General bag that held a bouquet of plastic flowers. That was another thing about being buried in Louisiana. The humidity was so high that real flowers would wilt in a matter of hours, so all you saw were gaudy plastic ones sprouting from stone vases and urns.

When we got there, I arranged the flowers, then knelt and kissed the name on the stone lid and prayed. When I lifted my head, I looked off toward the edge of the swamp. Something caught my eye beyond the edge of the willows, where water-logged cypress grew plentiful at the water's edge.

It looked like someone was standing there in the deepening shadows... watching us.

"Jaybo," I said, "look yonder."

My husband, tall and gray-bearded, looked where I nodded. He stared at the spot and shrugged. "What am I supposed to be looking at? I don't see nothing but bush and bramble."

I stood and walked toward the edge of the cemetery. The place where I'd seen the dark form was empty now. Just a stretch of marshy bank cast in shadow, framed by long beards of Spanish moss and thicket.

"Where are you going, Becky?" Jaybo asked. "Don't you be walking out there by yourself. You'll get snakebit... or a gator'll drag you under that nasty water and drown you!"

"Aw, quit your fussing!" I told him. I took it easy, stepping high through the kudzu and tall ferns. I'm slower and more cautious these days, since I had my hip surgery a couple of years ago. I'm far from the wiry, tree-climbing girl I was in my younger years.

When I reached the spot, I stood there and looked around. The channel of Black Bayou could be seen between the trees, quiet and dark, still as mysterious as it had been when I was a young'un. I looked down at the mossy earth and saw tracks. Not the tracks of a man, but longer and broader, with deep indentations where the tips of the toes should have been.

"See anything?" Jaybo walked up behind me and stood there, patiently. He knew I had to have my time, especially where the bayou was concerned, so he was gracious enough to give me that consideration.

"No...just these tracks here." I turned my head and something odd caught my attention. "And maybe that there."

High on the smooth trunk of a bald cypress, something was carved into the wood. I stared at it for a long moment, puzzling on why and how it had gotten there.

B.M. LOVES J.S.

I turned to Jaybo with a question in my eyes. "Did you...?"

He shook his head. "Nope. Not that I recollect. Besides, if I'd done it, it would have been J.S. LOVES B.M., not the other way around."

I knew he was right. I'd carved one identical to that one, forty-nine years ago. But it had been way back in Black Bayou, where we'd stopped so I could pee. The afternoon before night descended upon the swamp and three men had been horribly slaughtered on Bergeron's Bar.

I stared at the carving. It was a far piece above the ground... maybe six or seven feet high on the tree.

Seeing it, I couldn't help but smile. *It remembered,* I thought. *After all these years.*

"It's getting late, Becky," Jaybo complained. "And I'm getting hungry."

I nodded. "How about some catfish and white beans? Hushpuppies on the side?" We knew of a restaurant in the parish that served such delicacies.

"Sounds damn good to me," my husband agreed.

I took out my phone and snapped a picture of the crude carving on the tree for a keepsake. Before leaving, I spotted curls of fresh wood around the roots of the old cypress. The carving had been put there minutes before I got there.

I looked across the still waters of Black Bayou, searching, but finding no one. Or no *thing.*

"Thank you," I whispered, so low that Jaybo couldn't hear.

Then, taking his hand, we left the dank shadows and walked back to the car.

MOJO MAMA

Quite abruptly and without warning, a searing pain blossomed in the hollow of his throat, just above the junction of his collarbones. Quentin Devereaux reined his horse to a halt and coughed violently. He choked on the obstruction, feeling it move—of its own accord—up the narrow tube of his esophagus and into the chamber of his mouth. He sensed the motion of flailing legs and the tip of a stinger raking across the soft flesh of his palate. Then he spat, releasing the awful creature from its imprisonment. A small yellow-brown scorpion landed in the dust, then scampered off the pathway into the tall weeds.

The taste of blood and poison filled the young gentleman's mouth and he cursed. "Damn that black bitch!" he rasped. "Damn that Mojo Mama!"

Quentin sat in the saddle for a moment, regaining his composure and allowing the agony to fade from his throat. A few seconds later, the discomfort had subsided. But it would return. He knew that, deep down inside him, the potential for pain was endless.

The first time Quentin realized that the house of Devereaux was cursed was during the battle of Gettysburg. He had been leading his cavalry division in a charge against the Northern forces, when a horrendous pain had engulfed his stomach. At first, he thought he had been gut-shot by a Union bullet or skewered by the sword of a passing cavalryman. But when he examined himself, he found no evidence of a wound… no blood at all.

The pain, however, had increased tenfold. It grew so intense that he doubled over and fell from his saddle. While chaos surged around him, he was on his knees, cramping and gasping as the agony in his belly traveled up through the narrow channel of his throat. He opened his mouth to scream and watched, mortified, as a swarm of red wasps fluttered past his lips and took flight into the bullet-ridden air. He had wheezed for a long moment, his throat and mouth swollen from their attack, stingers spearing his inner flesh in a dozen or so places. Quentin was certain that he would suffocate, when the inflammation suddenly receded and, within moments, he was back to normal again.

He had suffered numerous attacks after that…from all manner of creatures and from the confines of his own traitorous body. It wasn't until the end of the War, just before the Confederate surrender at Appomattox, that Quentin had received a letter from his older brother, Trevor, informing him of the horrible curse that had been cast upon those unfortunate enough to share the Devereaux family name.

Quentin urged his steed forward, past the deserted slave cabins, to the run-down stable. An old Negro gentleman named Percy took the reins as he dismounted. Percy had been the last one to remain at the Devereaux sugar plantation. He was a free man but chose to stay out of convenience and a loyalty that the others had not felt toward their former masters. He eyed young Quentin curiously before leading the horse to its stall. "You've gots blood…" he said, pointing to the corner of his mouth. "Here."

Irritated, Quentin raised the back of his hand and wiped the trickle of blood away. "Never you mind."

As he started toward the stable door, Quentin felt Percy's eyes upon him. He could imagine the man smiling behind his back, perhaps in secret approval of the misery he and his siblings were enduring. But when he turned to confront the old uncle's glee, he found that he was already out of view, unsaddling the gelding and grooming its chestnut-brown coat.

Quentin took a cobbled walkway through the garden, toward the two-story manor. The once brilliant and well-kept *jardin des plantes*— as their Cajun-born mother had once called it—was now forlorn and choked with weeds. The circular pond in the center was covered over with a dense scum of green algae and the marble statues that their father had imported from Greece stood dismally around the courtyard, devoid of their former luster and stained with a heavy coating of thick, black mold.

He left the ruins of the garden and approached the main house. The Devereaux mansion had once been the finest in all Louisiana and their sugar plantation the most prosperous in the land. Then the War Between the States had come along and, fast upon its heels, the dreaded Curse of the Devereauxs. It wasn't long afterward that everything that the Devereaux family had built their life upon—health, wealth, and power—had fallen into a vicious cycle of affliction, poverty, and disrespect.

Quentin was almost to the mansion, when he heard the sound of mournful crying coming from a utility shed that stood away from the rear of the house. He hesitated for a long moment, torn between investigating the grievous sound or leaving the poor soul to their private misery. But, in the end, his love for his sister surpassed his own emotional discomfort.

"Isabella," he said softly when he reached the shack's wooden door. He knocked at the panel with his knuckles. "Isabella... are you alright?"

A cross between a harsh laugh and a ragged sob answered his foolish question. "No, Quentin, I most certainly am *not* alright! Now, go away and leave me alone."

"Please, Isabella... I must speak with you," Quentin insisted of his sister.

Inside the awful crying resumed, along with the sound of liquid falling into a metal basin...dripping, pouring, continuously. "No, Quentin. I'll not have you see me in such a way."

Quentin himself did not desire to see his sibling in such a sorrowful state of physical distress, but he knew that he must talk to her and try to understand the extent of the awful curse that they had been subjected to.

"I am coming in, Isabella," he said and slowly opened the door.

Despite her protest, Quentin entered the utility shed. The interior of the structure was dark and dusty, but the invasion of daylight revealed the horror within. His sister squatted, naked, within a large metal wash tub filled with blood.

It was Isabella's *own* blood that she was awash in. For that was his sister's part of the dreaded curse. Once a month, during her womanly menstruation, she did not merely bleed from her womanly portal, but from every orifice of her body, including the pores of her skin. And that was not the most horrible aspect of her ailment. To prevent herself from bleeding to death, she was forced to ingest that which her body depleted.

In an atrocious act of self-vampirism, poor Isabella had to drink her own blood in order to survive.

His sister sobbed as he entered. "Please, brother... cast your eyes from my shame."

Quentin did as she said, focusing on the earthen floor of the shed instead. It angered him to see his sister a victim of such an abominable infirmity. "Isabella, you have nothing to be ashamed of. Like Trevor and I, you are guiltless."

He listened to her dip a china cup into the sanguine pool around her and, with great thirst, swallow her own bodily fluids. The noise nearly made him retch. "My only crime is possessing the filthy name of Devereaux. It is our dear, departed patriarch who has brought this awful curse upon us all. I hope his heathen soul burns in Hell for all eternity!"

Her brother was shocked to hear her speak of their father in such a cruel manner. Isabella had once been Everett Devereaux's pride and joy, a "daddy's girl" in every way imaginable. But her current state of despair and grave illness had changed her opinion of him considerably.

"But what did our late father do to raise the witch's ire and bring such a heinous curse upon this family?" he asked. He lifted his eyes from the floor and looked at his sister. She sat there, blood dripping and dribbling from her nose, mouth, and ears. A steady stream coursed from both eyes, running down her alabaster cheeks like crimson tears.

"Did Trevor's letter not reveal to you the shame and depravity that our dear parents cast upon this house?" she asked. As she looked at him, her eyes widened. "Good God Almighty... Quentin!"

Isabella had glimpsed his own personal angst before he himself had felt the burning sting in his nasal passages. A long, black centipede exited from his left nostril, its multitude of legs clawing for release. It dropped to the floor, covered with blood and mucus. Quentin attempted to crush the offending insect beneath the heel of his boot, but it escaped, skittering across the dirt of the floor and vanishing into the dank shadows.

Quentin wiped the bloody snot from his nostrils... a gesture that was more habit now than from conscious intention. "No, he said only that father was dead and that Mojo Mama had placed a curse upon our family. He did not go into details."

Small, thin streams of blood squirted from Isabella's nipples. Humiliated, she folded her slender arms across her breasts and wept. "Then go and demand that he tell you all. I cannot bear to speak of the awful business myself!"

Quentin regarded his sister's pitiful form, sitting in a bath of congealing gore. "Isabella... if I could only reverse this horrid curse..."

"Perhaps you can, brother," she said. "But speak to Trevor first." She lowered her head. Blood pooled from the openings around the follicles of her ebony hair, turning her lovely mane into a nasty, purulent mess. "Now go. Abandon me to my own wretchedness."

Not knowing what to say to relieve her distress, Quentin quietly closed the door and turned toward the house. Anger flared within him. He knew he must confront Trevor and demand to know the extent of the purgatory into which they had been unwilling cast.

As he entered the rear door and made his way toward the main hall, he thought of how he had found the Devereaux mansion upon his return from war—run down, deserted of their trusted servants, and in a state of perpetual decay. His mother, Rosalinda, had been alive then, but only in a physical sense. Her mind—once so sharp and full of good humor—had retreated into itself. Quentin had found her in a stupor born of madness and intoxicated with liquor and morphine. She had scarcely recognized who he actually was. But, as far as he could tell, she had not been touched by the Curse of the Devereauxs... not with the horrible aliments that Quentin and his siblings suffered. No, her torment had come later... several nights after his unexpected return.

Quentin pushed the awful fate of his mother from his thoughts. He had more urgent questions on his mind at the moment. The young man pushed through the double doors of the grand parlor. "Trevor!" he called. "Trevor, I must speak to you at once!"

When he stepped through the doorway of the parlor, it felt as though he was entering the white-hot belly of a blast furnace. Despite the humidity and heat of the summer afternoon, Trevor kept the great marble fireplace stoked and blazing. But, then, his older brother had reason to keep the fire going from morning until night.

Cloaked in a dark, woolen blanket, Trevor turned and regarded him. "Then speak, brother. I am here... as I always shall be."

Quentin intended to approach his brother boldly and with no hesitation.

But the hideous stench of decay that filled the room caused him to gag and consider retreat. He stood his ground, however, and covered his nose with a handkerchief from his vest pocket. As he crossed the fire-lit chamber, he found thick mats of green flies and black gnats seething upon the velvet drapes and the cushions of the furnishings... waiting, hungering, but hesitant to approach the heat of the fire.

When he came within six feet of the form hunkered before the fire, Quentin stopped. He could draw no closer. Even where he stood, the bile threatened to roll from his belly and into his mouth. But he dared not vomit. To do so would bring a new nest of horrors from within him, and he was afraid such an expulsion would dampen the indignation he now directed toward his elder brother.

"I demand that you tell me all concerning this sordid business between the house of Devereaux and that witch in the swamp," he said. "What sin did our parents commit to bring such sorrow upon us?"

"What would the telling of the story resolve?" Trevor said sadly. "Best leave it in the darkness where it belongs."

"No!" snapped Quentin. "Tell me... if only for my own peace of mind."

Trevor laughed. "Peace of mind? That is hilarious, little brother. Never again shall our namesake enjoy such a luxury."

Quentin watched in disgust as Trevor's right hand emerged from beneath his cloak. The flesh of the appendage was raw and decayed. Plump white maggots teamed within the bloody meat, feeding, crawling along his skeletal fingers. Trevor stuck his hand into the crackling flames of the fireplace. Instantly, the larva sizzled and popped, and the exposed meat of his failing flesh turned black with cauterization... but only temporarily.

That was the elder Devereaux's personal curse--the constant decay of his outer skin and the muscle underneath. Beneath the woolen blanket, Quentin sat naked, his fingers and toes, even his manhood, rotted away, leaving gaping wounds. It was the same with his head and torso. Within the dark, bloody cavity of his chest and abdomen, his internal organs continued to function, though turning gelatinous from gangrene and infested with parasites and the eggs that would produce a thousand more.

Quentin tightened the cloth upon his nostrils. He felt the contents of his stomach threaten to rise, with the assistance of the creatures that grew and generated within the dark recesses of his own body. With much effort, he quelled the sickness that threatened to overcome him.

"Brother, I beg of you, tell me the truth," he said, his anger smoldering into despair. "Perhaps I can do something. Perhaps I can reverse this damnation that we have been subjected to."

Haughtily, Trevor cast back the hood of his cover. His face was a glistening red skull, devoid of hair or ears. His lips had rotted away, revealing strong white teeth that had once charmed the belles of the sugar district. It was true... Trevor had once been a dashing and handsome gentleman. But that was no longer evident, given his deteriorating condition.

"All right! If you must know, then I shall tell you!" His bloodshot eyes glared from the lidless pits of their sockets. Several blue-bottle flies had grown bold and lit atop the membrane-thin flesh of his skull. "It was all begat by adultery, dear brother. Debauchery and unbridled lust."

Quentin baulked. "But our father had no such tendencies!"

A look of disgust crossed Trevor's disfigured face. "Oh, it wasn't *he* who performed the offending act. Rather it was our dear, sweet mother."

Quentin's rage resurfaced. "Liar!"

"No, I speak the truth. It is a hard potion to swallow to be sure, but genuine nonetheless." Trevor straightened his leg and laid it upon the blazing logs of the fireplace. Soon, the stench of gangrene was replaced by the odor of rancid meat, cooked to the bone.

Heavily and with dread, Quentin sat on an ottoman. "Then tell me all that you know."

Trevor looked into the fire, as though seeing all that had transpired within the ebb and tide of the flames. "Unbeknownst to you, lovely and genteel Rosalinda Devereaux had a dark passion... a carnal desire for pleasure other than what was consummated in her marriage bed. She particularly hungered for the attention of the male slaves that Father worked from daybreak to dawn in the canebrake. One in particular held her fancy... a strong, young buck named Jonathan. You remember him, don't you? Nearly seven feet tall, strong as an oak and as black as pitch. And, crudely put, rather well-endowed. That was how our mother liked her taboo lovers... as strong and jolting as a cup of Mammy Sophia's fresh-brewed coffee."

Quentin felt an agonizing pain seize the center of his brain. He gasped aloud and felt the discomfort gravitate toward the side of his head, through the narrow channel of his left ear. He reached up as the invader emerged. With a curse, he pried an earwig free from the confines of his ear. Its long, jagged pinchers gnashed, coated with blood and brain matter, as Quentin flung it into the flames of the hearth.

Trevor chuckled softly, then continued. "Her clandestine affair with young Jonathan went on for several months. I was aware of it, for I had come across them in the forest east of the sorghum mill. They lay in a bed of Spanish moss, rutting like wild animals, our saintly mother on top, taking all that he had to offer. She saw me standing there in the shadows, watching, but it did not alarm her. Rather, it seemed to heighten her excitement. Afterward, I promised to keep her secret, knowing how our father would react to such an unseemly liaison."

"But he did find out?"

"Yes, several weeks later." An expression akin to lunacy shone from Trevor's eyes as he spoke. "He found them, naked and writhing, drenched with the sweat of their passion, on the floor of the smokehouse. Father went mad with rage. He flung mother toward the house, then prying an axe from a stump near the woodpile, decapitated his wife's dark lover. He gathered up some of the other slaves, threatened them into secrecy, and had them carry the body off into the swamp to be disposed of. He took Jonathan's head, impaled it on a fence post, and set it aflame to serve as an example for any others who might have provided Rosalinda with her shameful pleasure.

"Afterward, everything fell apart for the Devereaux family. Jonathan's elderly mother grieved for days. You could hear her wailing along the dark banks of the swamp, searching for a trace of her son's remains, intending to bury him in a respectful manner. But she never found him. His headless body had been concealed well, undoubtedly weighted down with stones and dropped into the quicksand pit at the far side of the bayou. A week later, she appeared on the front lawn of our house and did her dirty deed in retaliation for the murder of her only son."

"The curse," said Quentin, lifting his face from his hands.

Trevor nodded. "She was known among the darkies as Mojo Mama. A swamp witch well-versed in the ways of voodoo and black magic. They were all afraid of her, as our father should have been. But he merely laughed and ridiculed her from the upstairs balcony as she opened a brightly-beaded bag and began to lay a number of objects in the dust at the foot of the front steps: a chicken foot, possum bones, a black candle, and a fine white powder that she spread about in a circle. Then she uttered a series of incantations that would dissolve the reserve of the most stout-hearted man. Our father was foolish. He cursed at her from the balcony and threatened to kill her the same as he had Jonathan. Mojo Mama jabbed a bony, black finger at him and cursed him and all who had lived and been sired beneath the roof of the Devereaux house to an agonizing Hell on Earth. Then she went to the fence post, pried her son's blackened skull from its pinnacle, and disappeared into the swamp."

"What happened then?" Quentin asked, although he could only imagine the worst.

"For several days, nothing at all," said Trevor. "Father strutted about the house, making light of the witch's curse and even laughing about the beheading of our mother's Negro lover. Then it began to happen." His brother paused and stared at him. "You remember how our father was… strong and robust, beefy and as wide as the gate to mother's flower garden. Well, he began to waste away. Day after day, he lost pound upon pound of muscle, until he grew gangly and frail. He had Mammy prepare a bounty of food, but no matter how much he ate, he continued to dwindle down to nothing. Then his horror grew even more mortifying. His flesh decreased while his bones grew sharper and more pronounced. They began to break through his skin, exposed nakedly to the elements. One morning he did not come down for breakfast and we went up to find him lying in his bed, no more than a skeleton without flesh or innards. The only thing that remained were his eyes lying within the dry sockets of his skull, full of terror and remorse."

"Good Lord!" exclaimed Quentin. "Pray… continue."

Trevor did so, although with no pleasure. "After his death, about the time of the conflict at Gettysburg, our own individual curses came to be revealed. My putrescent state of decay, poor Isabella's monthly bleeding, and your own nasty condition. Our mother, however, did not seem to suffer. She remained in her room upstairs, indulging in brandy and narcotics, with the door firmly barred and locked. And there she remained, until the curse of Mojo Mama finally came calling on her in the dead of night. But I have no need to speak further. You were here, in this very house, during that grisly discovery at the stroke of midnight."

Quentin shuddered at the thought. But he did not wish to dwell on his mother's death at that moment. Rather he was intent on finding a solution to the dire situation they now endured. "I shall go to Mojo Mama and reason with her. I will try to convince her that we, as children of the Devereaux name, had nothing to do with her son's murder. Shall I saddle a horse so that you may accompany me?"

Trevor laughed bitterly. "Are you mad? Me, leave the confines of this house? Why, the beasts of the swamp—the boars and the buzzards, the gators and the gars—would lay waste to my decaying carcass before I rode a quarter mile into the bayou. It would be certain death for me!"

Quentin knew that his brother was correct. To take him into the swamp would be like ringing the dinner bell for every hungry creature south of the canebrake. He stood and went to a side table. Opening an upper drawer, he took out a Colt Navy revolver that he had taken off the body of a dead Yankee following the Battle of Stones River. He checked the cylinder of the 36-caliber pistol. It was packed with powder and lead and primed with percussion caps.

"Then I shall go alone and take my chances," he said boldly, gathering his nerve. "We must have relief from this ungodly curse!"

Trevor sighed. "The only relief we shall find, dear brother, is in Death's firm grasp. I grow weary and pray for it to come soon."

Quentin ignored his sibling's dark mood, shaking his head in resignation as Trevor turned back to the fire. If his brother was unwilling to reason with the old witch, then it was up to Quentin to go on his behalf. As he left the parlor, he turned to find that Trevor had stuck his head into the leaping wall of flames. He did not die, but screamed as the meat of his face and tongue blackened into living, breathing ash.

Daylight darkened into twilight as Quentin Devereaux rode along a narrow path through the heart of the swamp. His horse—which had weathered cavalry charges, cannon blasts, and the cries of dying soldiers—was skittish amid the dense thicket and the water-logged columns of cypress shrouded with stringy, gray moss. The bayou was heavy with unfamiliar sounds, as well. The crying of loons, the rustling of unseen creatures in the brush, and the distant bellowing of bull gators in search of their mates… or an unwary meal.

As Quentin rode along the trail, he recalled the night of his mother's death. It had been a humid evening, so sweltering that nearly every window in the house had to be opened. Still, there was no breeze and nary a current of fetid air stirred. It was as though the wind waited, expectantly, for some horrible event to occur before daring to ruffle a shred of curtain or cool the heat-dampened skin of a single inhabitant.

Quentin had lain in his bed, bathed in sweat, unable to sleep. Trevor and Isabella had retired early, dealing with their own private portions of the Curse of the Devereauxs. Quentin could feel worms, beetles, and only God knew what else scampering through his intestines. They moved, en masse, through the moist, warm darkness of his bowels, searching for a single ray of light that might provide direction to the outside world. But there was no moon that night. It was pitch black and his internal tormentors had no such luck.

It was nearing the hour of midnight, when he heard sounds echoing from the west wing of the mansion… where his mother's bedroom was located. They were not the fitful thrashings of a nightmare or the tearful grief a widow might express at the loss of her husband. No, these were low moans and purring sighs, the kind that suggested a passionate coupling. At first, he thought that Rosalinda was pleasuring herself. She indulged in the act, and with great abandon, when she drank heavily. But, no, Quentin could also discern the creaking of the bed frame, as if tested by some vast weight. He turned over on his pillow, intending to drive the shameful sounds from his ears, when they turned from pleasure to pain. His mother began to scream, crying for mercy, pleading for her attacker to stop. But the creaking of the bed continued. The ornately-carved headboard struck the wall behind it, again and again, rending delicate French wallpaper and battering plaster into dust.

Trevor and Isabella joined him in the hallway. By candlelight, they ran down the upstairs corridor, toward the western wing. A scream of immeasurable torment rang throughout the house but grew silent as they reached the door of Rosalinda's bedroom. They found the door locked and barred from the inside. It took them several minutes to find something heavy and sturdy enough to batter the oaken door from its frame, but eventually they succeeded.

When they entered the room, candles held before them, they made a discovery that would haunt them the rest of their lives. Their beloved mother lay limply across the blood-soaked bed. She was naked, her once-beautiful face now a rictus of horror and agony. Her pale abdomen had burst from crotch to breastbone, as though she had been split open from the inside out.

They had rushed to the open window to see a huge form, dark and glistening with sweat, running across the lawn, toward the black expanse of the swamp. The three thought that the lack of nocturnal light was playing tricks on their eyes. The escaping attacker seemed to possess nothing above his broad, muscular shoulders.

Since that night, Quentin and his siblings had not had an easy moment and their individual shares of the Curse of the Devereauxs seemed to grow stronger and more relentless. Now, heading into the swamp on a mission, Quentin hoped to end their distress once and for all.

The pathway gradually widened into a clearing and, suddenly, he found himself before the tin and tarpaper shack of Mojo Mama. The sagging porch of the structure bore fronds of dried herbs and swamp plants, obviously the ingredients to the various potions and poultices that she concocted. The tanned hides of rabbits, possums, and raccoons hung, stretched, across the outer walls of the old shack, along with the skins of critters that he could not identify.

He reined his horse to a halt and swung down from the saddle. "Come out here, old woman!" he demanded. "I am here to have words with you!"

For a moment, he thought that she was not there. Then the door of weathered planks swung back on leather hinges and she appeared.

"I believe I smell the stench of Devereaux in the air."

Mojo Mama was far from the imposing figure he expected to find. She was small and frail, no more than five feet tall, dressed in ragged clothing and a dark blue bandana around the crown of her head. She was old—at least in her eighties—and as wrinkled and lined as the bark of an ancient tree. Only her eyes looked bright and youthful, twinkling with both malice and amusement as she regarded him.

"I've come to—" Quentin began.

"Beg for my mercy?" she asked. "If that be so, you'd best get on back home to your suffering. The curse I've cast upon the house of Devereaux stands… and always shall stand."

The old woman's proclamation enraged Quentin. He started forward, his hands balled into angry fists. "Now, see here, witch! Can we not bargain for a resolution to this damnable grudge of yours?"

Mojo Mama laughed and smiled, revealing toothless gums as blue as a skink's tail. "Bargain? Did your hot-headed fool of a father give my poor Jonathan such a choice when he found him with your whore of a mother? Did he show compassion before he swung that broad-axe and cleaved my son's head from his shoulders?" She pointed toward the side of the yard with a gnarled finger. A wooden headstone stood in the weeds beneath a weeping willow tree. "All that he left for me to commend to earth lies there, severed and burnt, in the soil."

Quentin attempted to calm down and reason with her. "I promise, I will help you locate the rest of your son's remains, if only you will—"

Mojo Mama grinned and idly fingered a dried chicken foot that hung from a lanyard of gator teeth around her scrawny neck. "Oh, the remains of my beloved Jonathan are around here somewheres… lurking, hiding… *watching*."

The young man's anger flared once again. "You'd best not play games with me, bitch, or I'll—"

Eyes gleaming, Mojo Mama raised her left hand, her dark fingers curled toward the night sky. "Or you'll *what*, young Devereaux?"

Without warning, a horrible pain shot throughout Quentin. It was an agony unlike any he had ever felt before. Something long and sinuous began to travel up from the depths of his stomach, filling his throat and forcing itself into his mouth. Quentin fell to his knees and retched. In horror, he watched as the head of a snake pushed past his lips. It contorted within him as it struggled for escape. Soon, the last of it left him and dropped on the ground. It was a copperhead, perhaps two feet in length. It hissed at him with venomous fangs, then slithered off into the darkness of the swamp.

"Do you wish for me to conjure another?" she asked cruelly. "A rattler or a cottonmouth perhaps? You hold more than you could ever imagine."

Quentin staggered to his feet, his throat raw and bloody with the serpent's passage. "Why do you torment us so? We had nothing to do with our parents' sins. Why do you not leave us be?"

"Because you are Devereaux," she said firmly. "And, as long as I hold breath in my lungs, you shall know the horrors of Satan's lot within your own treacherous bodies."

"Then your lungs and yourself be damned!" declared Quentin. Angrily, he drew the Navy revolver from beneath his coat and thumbed back the hammer.

The witch simply stood there as he emptied the contents of the .36 pistol into her chest. She wavered on her feet for a long second, smiling at him as she belched blood and bullet-shredded tissue. Then she dropped to the boards of the porch, never to move again.

That should be it then, he told himself with satisfaction. *With the witch dead, then the curse shall be no more.*

Quentin Devereaux stepped into a stirrup of the gelding's saddle and swung astride. He looked at the crumpled form of Mojo Mama one last time, then with a scowl, headed back toward the bayou trail.

An hour passed. Two. Quentin began to realize that he had somehow taken a wrong turn. He was lost in the dangerous darkness of the swamp with no idea of where he was. The Devereaux plantation was to the north, but he could no longer discern which direction was which. The pale orb of a full moon hung overhead, visible through the Spanish moss and the gnarled limbs of the cypress trees, but somehow it seemed to shift at random, providing no aid to his bearings.

As he rode through a tall stand of wild canebrake, he suddenly heard the sound of something behind him. It was the noise of bare feet in the brush, moving stealthily like a cat. But he knew that it was no feline that pursued him. Its size was immense as it picked its way through the stand of bamboo. And that was not all that he heard. With the sound of footsteps came a peculiar whistling noise… like air forced through a narrow, wet opening.

Quentin urged his horse onward. The gelding grew skittish in the darkness, unable to see where it was going. The canebrake grew thicker, pressing in on the trail like opposing walls, making it difficult to navigate. The young man strained his ears for sound. He was thankful to find that he could no longer hear the sound of the footsteps... as well as the moist wheezing that accompanied them.

"Let's take leave of this damned place and get back home," he told his horse soothingly. His eyes peered into the darkness, trying to gauge his surroundings in the pale moonlight.

Abruptly, they were set upon. From out of the canebrake, two dark arms extended. Strong hands—calloused from grueling work at the urging whip of the overseer—grasped the throat of the gelding. With a powerful yank, the horse's neck was broken. Its eyes rolled into the back of its head and it dropped to its side, pinning Quentin Devereaux underneath.

Frightened, he struggled to pull himself free. He looked around frantically, but the arms of the demon in the canebrake had disappeared.

With some effort, Quentin managed to wiggle from beneath the weight of the dead animal. But something was wrong with his leg. He shrieked as he attempted to stand. Quentin looked down to see a jagged shard of bone protruding through his trousers, just below the knee.

He tried several times to walk but fell each time. "Lord help me!" he cried out, teeth clenched against the agony that throbbed through his shattered shinbone. "Please... deliver me from this hellhole."

Slowly, he began to crawl on his hands and knees along the muddy pathway between the towering stalks of sugar cane. It was slow going... one torturous inch at a time. Once a swamp adder slithered across his path, scarcely a foot from his nose. He nearly screamed, but he knew he didn't dare. It would only alert the wild creatures and gators, who hunted in darkness, searching for a helpless morsel such as himself, of his whereabouts.

He had only traveled a few yards when he heard something come crashing out of the canebrake. He rolled over onto his back to find the thing that had killed his horse, standing on the pathway eight feet away.

It was the headless body of Jonathan—naked, his ebony skin glistening with sweat and wet sand. The ugly hole within the column of his neck—severed just above the larynx—sputtered and wheezed as his lungs inflated and deflated without benefit of those cerebral impulses necessary for such function.

"No!" screamed Quentin. "Lord Jesus, no... it is impossible!"

But he knew that Mojo Mama's voodoo had made it possible. Out of love and vengeance, she had conjured a spell and turned the sunken remains of her only son into a living, breathing zombie. Horrified, he watched as the headless corpse started toward him. Its huge, dark hands clenched and unclenched angrily, ready to latch upon the murderer of the woman who had once given birth to him.

Quentin wailed and tried to crawl away. He dismissed the revolver in his coat, for in his haste he had neglected to bring powder and ball with which to reload. The youngest of the Devereauxs scrambled only a few feet, before hands roughly took hold of him. He wept, waiting to feel strong fingers close about his gullet, expecting the quick twist that might shatter his neckbone and send him spiraling into the dark void of death.

But it did not come. No, something much more horrifying took place. He felt the thing's brawny arms encircle him, lifting him from the pathway. Quentin shut his eyes in revulsion as it pressed him closely to its broad chest, almost tenderly so. He struggled to break free, but there was no chance of doing so.

Quentin pleaded as Jonathan headed through the canebrake with him in tow. Onward into the bayou it took him, until they reached a broad clearing amid a crescent of ancient swamp oaks. There the zombie took a few steps forward… and sank…returning to the mire of the quicksand pit it had been confined to following its untimely death.

Quentin screamed until the quicksand slowly sucked them both downward. But as they went under, he realized that he was not suffocating as he should. The Curse of the Devereauxs had not ended with the shooting of Mojo Mama. It continued, even more terrifying than before.

Sinking toward the pool's murky bottom, Quentin Devereaux knew that he would spend eternity in a heightened state of torment and mortification, unable to die, trapped in the unyielding arms of the victim of his father's unbridled jealousy and rage.

As he hung there, suspended between life and death, he felt the creatures within him panic and surge into battle. Snake against toad, scorpion against spider, a nest of hornets against an invading army of angry red ants. All converged within him, biting, stinging, bringing agony and boundless fear… but, alas, no promise of finality.

BILLY BUD RECOGNIZED THE SPOT RIGHT AWAY.
IT WAS THE SAME PLACE THE GRANDSTAFF'S
HAD HELD THEIR FAMILY REUNION IN MAY.

BUT THE EVENT THAT WAS PLAYING OUT ON THE
SCREEN WAS NO FAMILY REUNION... NOT BY A
LONG SHOT.

THERE WERE MAYBE TWENTY-FIVE OR THIRTY PEOPLE
STANDING AROUND IN LONG, BLACK ROBES. THEY WORE
HALLOWEEN MASKS AND HELD BLACK CANDLES. THERE
WERE FRANKENSTEIN AND THE CREATURE FROM
THE BLACK LAGOON, AND CELEBRITIES, TOO. MARILYN
MONROE, RICHARD M. NIXON, EVEN ELVIS.

THE FINAL FEATURE

"Billy Bud!" hollered Big Vern, banging on the ceiling of the concession stand with a mop handle. "Get the wax outta your ears, boy!"

"Yeah, Daddy?" In the projection booth above, Billy Bud had been reading an old dog-eared copy of *Fangoria* in the flickering light of Projector Number One.

"I forgot and left the reel for the second feature at the house," his father told him. "Run over there right quick and get it, will you? It's on the kitchenette table."

"Yes, sir!"

Billy Bud Grandstaff laid his magazine aside and looked over at Projector Number Two. His father was right. The contraption was empty, no second feature reel on it at all. Wasn't like his papa to be so forgetful. No, that was pretty much *his* job.

He opened the steel door of the projection booth, made his way down the concrete steps, and hightailed it to the "house", as his papa called it. It was more like a single-wide trailer located at the back property line of the drive-in theatre lot. A rusty, white-and-aqua Fleetwood from the Sixties, perched precariously atop cinderblock columns.

Billy Bud was Vern Grandstaff's only son and not a very bright one at that. Big Vern bragged, almost proudly, that Billy Bud wasn't the sharpest lawn mower blade in the shed, and he reckoned he couldn't deny it. After all, he was forty-three, still living at home with his daddy and mama, and working the only job he had ever had: running the projectors at Big Vern's Drive-In off Highway 1, just west of the Atchafalaya River Bridge.

Halfway to the trailer, Billy Bud glanced back over his shoulder. They were showing a double feature that night. *Fast and Furious 11* and *Madagascar 6*, that movie with the talking lion and zebra and the fat lady hippo that looked sort of hot, if you squinted your eyes a bit.

Fast and Furious was fifteen minutes away from finishing up. It was the other one Big Vern had forgotten to load into the second projector that afternoon.

He bounded up the steps—also constructed of cinderblocks—and ducked inside. The inside was stuffy and stank of sweat, cigarette smoke, and unwashed laundry. Billy Bud went to the kitchenette table. Dirty dishes, ashtrays, and empty Budweiser cans littered its surface... but no flat, plastic case containing *Madagascar 6*. "Damn," he muttered. "Where in tarnation is it?"

Billy Bud looked all over the place, but it was nowhere to be found. If he'd actually thought for a moment and looked *under* the table, he would have found that it had slipped off the edge and joined bread crumbs and fossilized macaroni-and-cheese noodles on the dusty Formica floor.

"Billy Bud!" yelled his father from the direction of the concession stand. "Get that movie and get your ass back to the booth! It's almost intermission time!"

That was when Billy Bud did what he did best... he panicked. He knew if he didn't have something, *anything*, on Projector Number Two when the last-call-for-refreshment bell was rung, Big Vern would tan his hide. True, Billy Bud was middle-aged himself, but that wouldn't stop his daddy none.

In desperation, he left the trailer and went to the shack out back. Inside, he pulled a ceiling chain and a sixty-watt bulb snapped on. The shed was where Big Vern kept all his old movies. Not the new releases he rented every two weeks, but the ones he had bought and played back during the Seventies and Eighties, when the Drive-In was at its heyday. One set of shelves held old horror and science-fiction films like *Night of the Iguana Man*, *Grandson of the Iguana Man*, *Killer Gnats*, and *Booger-Eating Zombies from Planet 69*. A second set of shelves held Big Vern's exploitation films—the ones Billy Bud's mother didn't care much for. Movies like *Big-Boobed Biker Babes*, *Prison Pussy Party*, and Billy Bud's personal favorite, *I Was a Teen-Aged Meth-Whore*.

But none of those would do tonight. There were a lot of families on Friday nights, with a ton of kids. *Staple Gun 5* or *Bad Girls with Bullwhips* wouldn't be appropriate.

"Billy Bud... where the hell are you, boy?" Big Vern's voice sounded mad enough to chew nails and shit thumbtacks.

On top of an old Frigidaire was a wooden crate full of old cartoons. Droopy Dawg, Popeye the Sailor Man, Heckle and Jeckle. Billy Bud loved Heckle and Jeckle, but Big Vern didn't. He said they were just a couple of smart-ass birds, up to no good.

Billy Bud got down the crate, digging through it, looking for something he could play that wouldn't offend anybody, least of all his daddy. When he got to the bottom of the crate, he found a black metal reel that he'd never laid eyes on before. A strip of masking tape in the center read: *Black Mass, July 16, 2018.*

"BILLY BUD!" Big Vern's voice carried across the drive-in lot like the wrath of God. "Get back here with that movie… PRONTO!"

When Big Vern said "pronto" it was like the warden of death row asking "What would you like to order for your last meal? Fried chicken or meatloaf?"

"Aw… shit!" Billy Bud picked up the black reel, tucked it under his arm, and headed back to his post.

On his way, he saw that the ending credits of *Fast and Furious 11* were almost finished and folks were leaving their cars and trucks and gravitating toward the concession stand for round two of watered-down cold drinks and artery-clogging chili-cheese-fries.

Billy Bud bounded up the steps to the projection booth and slammed the door. As Projector One wound down, he popped the black reel on the spindles of Projector Two and pushed the auto-thread button. Big Vern had paid a pretty penny for the two high-tech projectors, both of them Super-Adapt 5000s. They would take any millimeter film, from 8mm to the kind today's movies were printed on. The one on the black reel was a 16mm, but the Super-Adapt worked like a pro, the spindles shifting inward, converging, and threading the slotted celluloid with no hassle at all. True, his father had paid $25,000 for the pair of them, while their septic tank was so backed up that they had to take a piss through a hole Vern had cut in the floor… but his father had assured them that it was an investment that simply couldn't be passed up.

As Billy Bud let Projector Two prepare itself for showtime, he looked out one of the projection holes that had been cut in the cinderblock wall. Directly in front of him was parked the Baxters' red Dodge dually. Usually, Greg and Thelma Baxter were sound asleep in the cab by the second feature, while their twin boys, Jimmy Jack and Johnny Joe lay, on their bellies, atop the truck's extended roof. The two ten-year-olds were there now, already decked out in their pajamas: Incredible Hulk for one and WWE Wrestling for the other.

Down below, he could hear his father at the concession stand register, hee-hawing loudly. Billy Bud frowned. The old man was probably flirting with Rhonda Sue Hickey, who did hair over at the

Bun, Bush, & Beard. Big Vern was always coming on to the girl, who was twenty-nine to his eighty-three, and showed his lust openly and unashamedly, before sending her on her way with a grilled cheese sandwich, onion rings, and Diet Fresca. Billy Bud's mother endured her husband's indiscretion with a grain of salt, too busy flipping footlongs and black angus patties on the grill in back to scold him.

After the last-call bell rang, the second feature was ready to begin. *Well, it ain't what the doctor ordered,* thought Billy Bud, *but here goes.*

He snapped on the auto-play switch and the film began to roll.

There was no title and no sign of credits. The picture on the big sixty-foot screen was blurry at first, then came sharply into focus. The scene was at night, but the flickering glow of patio tiki torches gave off enough light to reveal what was going on. Billy Bud recognized the spot right away. It was Shelter #14 over at Pomme De Terre State Park near Sutton Lake, the same place the Grandstaffs had held their annual family reunion last May.

But the event that was playing out on the screen was no family reunion... not by a long shot.

There were maybe twenty-five or thirty people standing around the shelter in long, black robes. They wore rubber Halloween masks and held black candles. Billy Bud studied the masked figures. There were Frankenstein and the Creature from the Black Lagoon, and celebrities, too. Marilyn Monroe, John F. Kennedy, Richard M. Nixon, even Elvis.

The camera panned to the right as the procession of robed folks congregated between two maple trees. Trussed up with clothesline and hung overhead was a bluetick coonhound, confused and whimpering pitifully.

The twin boys on the roof of the dually watched the opening scene intently.

"Hey, ain't that Luke Broussard's dog, Ol' Blue?" asked Jimmy Jack.

"I thought he got run over by a tractor-trailer on the interstate a while back," replied Johnny Joe.

The scene continued, getting weirder by the moment. The people in the long, black robes suddenly stripped down to nothing.

"Lordy Mercy!" said Johnny Joe. "Them folks are plumb buck-ass nekid!"

His brother nodded. "As the proverbial jaybird, I'd say."

Marilyn, a young woman, and Nixon, a much older man, stepped beneath Ol' Blue's squirming form. A man wearing a Wolfman mask held a long butcher knife over his head, then slit the poor pooch open from breastbone to balls. Marilyn and Nixon stood beneath a shower of dog blood, rubbing it all over themselves with great abandon.

Luke Broussard jumped out of his Ford pickup a few rows up ahead. He looked more than a mite *disturbed*. He began to march past the other cars, fists balled into angry white knots, heading toward the concession stand.

Billy Bud turned his eyes back to the screen. The other naked folks were catching the remaining torrent of Ol' Blue's life's blood in big Styrofoam cups with BIG VERN'S DRIVE-IN THEATRE printed on the side. They were the 48-ounce size—Vern's Super Slurp Special—so they held quite a lot.

Some of the drive-in patrons had begun to leave their cars now. Some seemed bumfuzzled by the whole thing. Others seemed outraged, and others seemed... well, they seemed downright embarrassed. The looks on their faces revealed that they weren't necessarily bothered by the gore or indecency of the scene that unfolded... but more by the *familiarity* of it all. Some started toward the concession stand, while others jumped back into their cars and revved their engines.

The scene on the screen had taken a turn for the worse. Nixon was getting it on with Marilyn now, rubbing his hands all over her blood-slickened skin. She had two large brass rings dangling from her nipples. Nixon reached around, hooked his knuckles in the rings, and gave them a hearty yank.

"Ouch!" said Jimmy Jack. "I bet that smarted!"

"Like King Kong's hangnail," countered Johnny Joe. Both boys grinned, amazed at how far human skin could actually stretch.

Suddenly, Big Vern was standing in the gravel lane down below, shaking his fist in the air. "What the shit have you done, Billy Bud?" His nose was bloody and out of alignment where Luke Broussard had nailed him. "Turn that crap off... NOW!"

Enthralled, Billy Bud continued to watch the movie. "Hey, Daddy... that feller in the Nixon mask has a gall bladder scar a lot like yours. *Just like yours*, to tell the truth."

Big Vern did a little dance of rage in the gravel. "I said shut that thing off... PRONTO!"

His father had said the word to end all words, but Billy Bud ignored him. Even in the face of his elder, he adhered to the Number One Rule of Drive-In Projection Maintenance and Operation. His father's stern command was etched into his brain, never to be banished. *"Son, always remember... no matter what...whether it rains or snows, whether a Tennessee tornado rips through sucking earth or Lord Jesus comes back*

*riding a winged Pegasus with the heavenly trumpets a-blaring... never...
I repeat, NEVER...turn that projector off in the middle of a showing."*

And that was exactly what Billy Bud took to heart now. He let the
projector do its thing, displaying every gory and horny detail upon that
big drive-in screen.

A loud crack like a rifle shot sounded as Rhonda Sue hauled off and
slapped the shit out of Big Vern. Then she marched off to her Honda
Accord, red-faced and indignant. Her ample breasts bounced beneath
her Lynyrd Skynyrd t-shirt, jingling like Santa's sleigh bells.

"I'm coming up there, boy," shouted Big Vern. Rhonda Sue's
handprint blazed across his left cheek like a five-fingered birthmark.
"And after I bust that projector, I'm gonna bust your sorry ass!"

Billy Bud stepped over, bolted the steel door of the projection booth,
and then went back to watching the movie. The naked folks had poured
the Super Slurps of blood all over a wooden picnic table, which had
been turned into a makeshift altar of some kind. Marilyn Monroe had
laid herself out, spread-eagled, while Nixon climbed on top of her. Billy
Bud thought that was just downright wrong. It should have been the
man in the JFK mask giving her a poke.

"What the shit is going on?" demanded Greg Baxter, haven woken
from his nap in the dually. "What're you showing here, Grandstaff...
pornoscopic movies? My young'uns don't need to watch this trash!"

"I don't mind," said Jimmy Jack.

"Me, neither," added Johnny Joe.

"You boys get in this here truck!" Thelma Baxter said, dragging the
twins off the top of the cab.

"Aw, Mama....!"

"And shut your eyes, for Heaven's sake!" She wrestled the pair into
the back seat of the Dodge and slammed the door.

Billy Bud returned his attention to the screen. Marilyn was on her
hands and knees now. A lanky white dude with a firefighter's emblem
tattooed on his butt cheek, wearing a Bozo the Clown mask, was
stepping up to take a turn.

Glen Oakley, the local fire chief, ground gears for a frantic moment,
before speeding off, carrying the mobile movie speaker with him.

That was when all hell broke loose. Cars and pickups started taking
off, one by one, slinging dust and gravel in the air. Others stuck around,
anxious to see if they could identify various tattoos, moles, and scars.

Big Vern was at the projection booth door, whaling away at the lock
with a ball-peen hammer.

A loud crash echoed from the far side of the lot. The mayor and the county sheriff had suffered a hellacious fender-bender, trying to be the first ones out of the exit gate.

Damn, thought Billy Bud, picking up his monster magazine and hunkering down on his stool. *Maybe I should have picked Heckle and Jeckle after all.*

EMBRACE

"Daaaaad!" Tina's voice was insistent... almost agonizingly whiney. The seven-year-old could be like that when she was tired and beyond boredom. Especially during long drives.

"I know, I know," her father told her. He looked over at her mother and rolled his eyes. "You're a) thirsty, b) hungry, or c) need to go to the bathroom. Right?"

The little girl's eyes narrowed as she studied the back of her father's head. "Uh-huh. But how did you know?"

"Because *I'm* thirsty, *I'm* hungry, and *I* need to pee like Snoodle the Doodle when he's had a bowlful of water!"

Tina giggled. The thought of Dad hiking his leg and watering a bush or mailbox post tickled her and she laughed some more. Then their Goldendoodle and his welfare came to mind and she frowned. "Do you think Snoodle is okay? Do you think he misses us?"

"I'm sure he does, baby," said Mom. "We've been gone for four days. I'm sure he's ready to bust out of that kennel and snuggle with you when we get home."

Dad grumbled. "That is, if we *ever* get home. We've been on this stretch of highway for nearly an hour now." Their return drive home from visiting his mother in New Iberia to their home in Alexandria had abruptly turned from a leisurely trip to a journey off the beaten path. Due to a nasty pile-up between a semi-truck and several cars that had slowed down due to road construction, they had been detoured off the busy thoroughfare of Interstate 49 onto the rural, two-line backroad of Highway 71 North. And, so far, they had seen no signs directing them back to the interstate. Mom had tried to pull up Google Maps on her phone, but there was no cell service to speak of way out there in the Louisiana sticks.

Tina's stomach grumbled hungrily and she sighed, looking out the side window of the car. All she saw was dark thicket and heavy forest. Sometimes there were broad stretches of swampland that looked full of snakes and toads… maybe even alligators.

"I don't think we've ever been anywhere without places to eat," she pouted. "Not even a danged McDonald's!"

"You're probably right," Dad told her. "Maybe we can find a store somewhere and grab us a snack. Then we'll get you a Happy Meal when we get to Alexandria."

"I think we might be in luck," Mom told them. "Look!"

At the roadside was a billboard framed in thick-leaved kudzu. It read:

WAYNE & ESTELLE'S STOP AND GO
GAS—GROCERIES—LIVE BAIT
STOP BY FOR AN RC COLA & MOON PIE!
2 MILES AHEAD!

"See!" said Dad, winking at her in the rearview mirror. "I know you like Moon Pies, especially the banana ones."

"Well, it ain't chicken nuggets and fries, but a Moon Pie would be okay. Can I have a Dr Pepper, though? RC makes me belch."

"You got it, pumpkin."

A few minutes later, they passed a white, steepled church house and several old houses with magnolias in their front yards. Off the highway and to the left was the Stop & Go.

The place wasn't much to look at, but the sign they had passed a while back had described it accurately, just a little mom and pop grocery with a couple of gas pumps out front. On the front porch was a couple of rocking chairs, a freezer with bags of ice, and two tanks with live bait. Minnows and nightcrawlers for fishing.

Dad parked their car in a spot at the side of the store and cut the engine. "Why don't we all get out and stretch our legs? See if they have a restroom we can use."

Mom and Tina climbed out of the car, while Dad laid his sunglasses on the top of the dash and checked his phone. Still no service. "I was hoping we could call the kennel. They close in forty-five minutes. If we don't get home soon, poor ol' Snoodle might have to stay another night in the hoosegow."

"Doggy resort, dear," Mom corrected, giving him a warning look.

"I sure hope not," said Tina, beginning to worry. "I know Snoodle is homesick. Just like me."

"We'll take a bathroom break, grab us a snack, and be back on the road in no time," her father assured. "I'm sure we'll get there in time."

They crossed the gravel lot and stepped up onto the store's front porch. The bare boards beneath their feet creaked as they walked past the rocking chairs and live bait tanks. They entered the store and found the place to be darker and cooler than it was outside. A dark-haired woman with black-framed eyeglasses stood at the register behind the counter.

"Howdy do, y'all!" she greeted as they walked in.

Dad squinted his eyes, allowing his eyes to adjust to the gloom. "You must be Mrs. Estelle."

"That I be," she replied. "I reckon you saw the sign a couple miles ago."

"We did," said Mom. "Would you have a restroom we could use?"

"Sure do. At the back of the store yonder. Help yourself."

"And we're hankering for some nourishment, too," Dad said. "Drinks and Moon Pies for us all."

Estelle laughed. "Well, now, don't know how nourishing they are, but we've got Pies aplenty. Chocolate, vanilla, banana. The cold drinks are in the coolers along the wall there."

While Mom and Tina visited the ladies' room, Dad gathered their beverages and food and paid for them. When mother and daughter returned, it was Dad's turn to visit the "little boy's room", as he put it.

"Sure been a bunch of traffic through here the past couple of hours," said the store owner. "Y'all know what's going on?"

As Mom began to tell her of the wreck on the interstate, Tina stood at the screen door and stared at the rusty gas pumps out front. Suddenly, she heard something. Something near the two weathered rockers on the porch.

Meow.

"Mom!" Tina called, interrupting her. "I hear a cat."

Estelle smiled and shook her head. "Honey child, there ain't no cats around here. Haven't been for years, as far as I know. They're too scared of the swamp critters hereabouts."

Meow! This time the cry was more urgent, almost as if it was alarmed.

"See! There it is again. It *is* a cat!"

She looked over her shoulder and saw that the two women were too busy talking to pay her any attention. "Mom!" she said louder, "I'm gonna go outside until Daddy's done, okay?"

Mom looked over at her and nodded. "Alright. But just stand there on the porch, okay?"

"You listen to your mama now, girl," Estelle advised. "Don't you go around back or nothing. Sometimes gators come up out of the thicket, looking for squirrels and such. Wouldn't want you to get bitten or worse."

"Yes, ma'am," promised Tina. "I won't."

She stepped outside and let the screen door slap shut behind her. She walked down the length of the porch, holding her nose as she passed the stinky vats of minnows and earthworms. When she reached the twin rocking chairs, she was certain she caught a fleeting glimpse of movement at the corner of the porch near the ice machine.

Meow.

There it is again! she thought to herself. *That old woman don't know what she's talking about. There is a cat. I knew it!*

Tina walked to the edge of the porch and stood there for a moment, listening. The cry of a cat came again, but at a distance now. She looked around the corner and saw motion in the high grass beyond the side wall of the little roadside store. Beyond the back corner was a stretch of weedy yard and a dark forest a half-acre or so away. Before the yard gave way to dense thicket, there was a huge, spreading oak tree. About the biggest one Tina had ever seen in her young life.

Yeeeoww! This time the sound of the cat was different. Louder and shriller… like it was frightened or hurt.

"What's wrong, kitty?" she called out. She studied the big oak and saw a flash of pale motion on one of the lower branches of the tree. "Are you stuck or something?"

She looked back at the screen door of the country store. She could still hear her mother and Mrs. Estelle talking up a blue streak, as her grandma in New Iberia was fond of saying. She wrestled with the promise she'd made a few moments before, then abandoned it when the animal cried out in pain again. Against her better judgment, she hopped off the porch and ran around the back of the building, toward the black oak tree.

Carefully, the seven-year-old made her way through the weeds toward the base of the tree. She watched for things that might be creeping or slithering in the high grass. She wished Snoodle the Doodle was there with her. He wouldn't let any stupid snakes or gators get hold of her.

Tina made it to the tree safely. The massive size of the tree was much more evident close up than it was at a distance. Roots as thick and big around as her father's arms protruded from the earth. The trunk of the oak was nearly as wide as their car was long. The wood was deeply etched and the color of coffee without cream. Knotholes and swirling patterns in the coarse bark of the trunk almost made it look like the tree had a face. An ancient, old man's face that grinned at her sinisterly the closer she approached.

Don't be scared, she told herself. *It's nothing but an old tree. It's just a... what do they call it? An optimal illusion."*

YEEEEEOW!

She looked up to the big limb that drooped six feet or so above her head. She could see that the animal's tail was visible now. The cat was a calico. The fur on its thrashing tail was a mixture of white, black, and orange.

Without hesitation, Tina stuck her fingertips into the deep groves of the bark, as well as the toe of her right sneaker. "Don't worry, kitty. I'll climb up and save you!" Then, inch by inch, she began to scale the trunk of the tree.

It took her a minute, but she finally reached the big limb. With some effort, she hoisted herself up and sat there, trying to catch her breath. She looked over and was surprised to find a large opening just above the junction where the limb jointed the tree trunk. The tail swayed back and forth frantically from the depths of the dark hollow.

Meeeow! The animal seemed less distressed now, as though hearing her voice had calmed it down a little.

She scooted down the length of the limb on her butt, hoping her jeans didn't get too dirty. She was in enough trouble already, just leaving the porch like she had.

Soon, she was there at the mouth of the hollow trunk.

"Hey there, kitty," she whispered, soothingly. "Don't be scared."

Tina reached out to pet the frightened animal.

But it wasn't a cat. Perhaps it had been one once... warm and alive, snoozing on couch cushions or hunting mice in the musky shade beneath porches or the dappled darkness of back-acre barns. All that was left now was tri-color fur and dried skin, stretched taut, across branches and twigs. False and deceptive.

"What the he—" She caught herself before she could say the word, the one Dad said when he stubbed his toe or hit his thumb with a hammer. "Heck?"

Suddenly, she found herself slipping... *pushed?*... into the gaping maw of the hollow tree. She let out a small, startled cry... but one much too weak and low to reach the store near the highway.

Falling downward, she grasped desperately with her small fingers.

Her palms raked the inner walls, drawing splinters and prickles of pain. For a moment Tina found herself dropping dizzily through pitch darkness. Then she found herself immersed... not in water, but something much thicker and heavier. Sticky, like pancake syrup...but dark and cold.

Tina struggled for breath, but the liquid plugged her nostrils and pressed against her lips. Smothering, she knew that if she opened her mouth, the cloying substance would fill her throat and lungs. As she flailed blindly, yearning for air, something bumped into her. Something small. Then again. A little bigger this time.

She felt a presence, there in the liquid, with her. A single word echoed through Tina's thoughts in her own voice. *Sister.*

An instant before she could drown, her head broke the surface of the gelatinous pool and she gasped, desperately drawing in frantic gulps of air. It was dark in the hollow of the tree, the way a cave might be... or the inside of a refrigerator with the door tightly shut. The hole overhead—the one she had fallen through—seemed to have healed itself.

Again, Tina felt as if someone was there in the tree with her. As the thick liquid around her receded, draining... she felt someone reach out and take her hand. At first the grasp was hard and unyielding, like the caress of a skeleton's fingers. Then it softened and grew warmer.

A tiny crack in the trunk of the tree parted, revealing a thread of sunshine. The glow ran vertically for several feet, then the seam broke open, slowly flooding the tree's belly with light. Revealing the thing that held her hand.

When she realized what it was, she opened her mouth to scream. But a nimble cord—*vine? root?*—encircled her throat, cutting off the cry before it could fully form.

The thing stretched and flexed, as though testing new muscle and nerve... fresh bone and the joints that linked them. The roundness of its face, the set of its ears, its features were intimately familiar... but horribly alarming. Black-pupiled eyes studied her until they, themselves, lightened and mimicked the azure hue of her own. Then dark flesh paled, grew the texture of hair and clothing, and it stood before her smiling.

Again, the word came. *Sister.* But it was from the lips of the imposter... formed in her own voice.

Soundlessly, the split in the tree broadened. The thing turned away from her and squeezed through, dropping to the ground wetly, as if departing the shelter of a womb. It stood and shivered in the shade cast by the boughs of the oak. Then it stepped boldly into the summer sun.

As the seam in the trunk slowly closed, Tina could see her mother and father rounding the corner of the store.

"Tina!" her mother called out. "We've been looking all over for you!"

The thing that looked like her… the *new* Tina… shuddered and walked toward them. "I… I tripped. Fell in a puddle. I'm all wet!"

Dad ran up and, despite her dampness, cradled her small form in his strong arms. "You're shivering, pumpkin! Let's get you back to the car."

"I… I'm… c-cold!"

"There's a throw in the trunk you can snuggle up in, baby," Mom told her. "You'll be warm in no time."

The true Tina thrashed and tried her best to break free, but found her wrists and ankles firmly held. Her small heart pounded wildly in her chest with panic.

"Mom… Dad…" Her voice was dry and rasping, scarcely a whisper.

The vine around her throat tightened. *Hush, child.*

Tears rolled down her freckled cheeks as she watched through the healing crack in the trunk. Mom and Dad leading the wrong Tina away, each holding a pale, wet hand. Reaching the car, opening the door, wrapping her in the fluffy pink throw from the trunk, placing her in the back seat, belting her in.

For an instant, the imposter looked her way and grinned, as though saying *I'm you.*

Then the vehicle pulled onto the two-line highway and was gone.

The thing that had once been Tina wept as tiny roots took hold, piercing cloth and flesh, gently and slowly coursing through tender veins. Cells hardened and tissue grew coarse and gray. The core of her muscles became rigid, festooned with the rings of her age and flowing vessels of sluggish sap.

As the sky darkened and crickets began to sing, all thoughts of school, friends, and home … of Mom, Dad, and Snoodle the Doodle… grew dull and without substance, as though they had never been. Instead, there were only dreams of bark and leaves, of the new life of spring, the fire of autumn, and the bitter, biting cold of winter.

And the firm and endless embrace of ancient oak.

ABOUT THE AUTHOR

Ronald Kelly was born November 20, 1959, in Nashville, Tennessee, where he was raised a Southern Baptist. He attended Pegram Elementary School and Cheatham County Central High School (both in Ashland City, Tennessee) before starting his writing career.

Ronald Kelly began his writing career in 1986 and quickly sold his first short story, "Breakfast Serial," to Terror Time Again magazine. His first novel, Hindsight was released by Zebra Books in 1990. His audiobook collection, Dark Dixie: Tales of Southern Horror, was on the nominating ballot of the 1992 Grammy Awards for Best Spoken Word or Non-Musical Album. Zebra published seven of Ronald Kelly's novels from 1990 to 1996. Ronald's short fiction work has been published by Cemetery Dance, Borderlands 3, Deathrealm, Dark at Heart, Hot Blood: Seeds of Fear, and many more. After selling hundreds of thousands of books, the bottom dropped out of the horror market in 1996. So, when Zebra dropped their horror line in October 1996, Ronald Kelly stopped writing for almost ten years and worked various jobs including welder, factory worker, production manager, drugstore manager, and custodian.

In 2006, Ronald Kelly started writing again. Since then, he has written and published several new novels (Hell Hollow, Restless Shadows, and The Buzzard Zone), numerous short story collections, and has become an elder statesman of Southern-Fried Horror in his chosen genre. In 2021, his collection of extreme horror tales, The Essential Sick Stuff, won the Splatterpunk Award for Best Collection. He is currently working on The Saga of Dead-Eye, a five-volume horror western series.

Ronald Kelly currently lives in a backwoods hollow in Brush Creek, Tennessee, with his wife and young'uns.

BOOK LIST

Novels

Blood Kin
Father's Little Helper (re-released as *Twelve Gauge*)
Fear (Author's Preferred Edition)
Hell Hollow
Hindsight
Moon of the Werewolf (re-released as Undertaker's Moon)
Pitfall
Restless Shadows
Something Out There (re-released as *The Dark'Un*)
The Buzzard Zone
The China Doll
The Possession (re-released as Burnt Magnolia)
The Saga of Dead-Eye, Book One: Vampires, Zombies, & Mojo Men
The Saga of Dead-Eye, Book Two: Werewolves, Swamp Critters, & Hellacious Haints
Timber Gray

Novellas

Flesh Welder

Collections

After the Burn
Cumberland Furnace and Other Fear Forged Fables
Dark Dixie
Dark Dixie II
Haunt of Southern-Fried Fear
Irish Gothic: Tales of Celtic Horror
Long Chills
Midnight Tide & Other Seaside Stories
Mister Glow-Bones & Other Halloween Tales
More Sick Stuff
Season's Creepings: Tales of Holiday Horror
Tales from the Southern-Fried Crypt
The Essential Sick Stuff
The Halloween Store and Other Tales of All Hallows' Eve
The Sick Stuff
The Web of La Sanguinaire and Other Arachnid Horrors
Twilight Hankerings
Unhinged

Curious about other Crossroad Press books?
Stop by our site:
http://store.crossroadpress.com
We offer quality writing
in digital, audio, and print formats.